KU-090-409

XB00 000015 3083

Buffalo Falls

Northern Texas, July, 1878: ex-cavalrymen Amos Kane and Luke Fisher end a hard, three-day ride when they reach the frontier town of Buffalo Falls, where the Farmer's Mercantile Bank is expecting an unusually large and secret cash shipment: $50,000.

Kane and Fisher arrive hoping to get taken on as drovers, but are offered the positions of marshal and deputy marshal instead. They accept, unaware that a gang of ruthless outlaws led by Everett and Jeb Stark know about the payroll.

Soon after the Starks ride into town, Kane and Fisher have a run-in with one of their gang. They then discover the real reason for the outlaws' visit . . . and the stage is set for violent confrontation.

Buffalo Falls

Robert B. McNeill

ROBERT HALE · LONDON

First published in Great Britain 2012

ISBN 978-0-7090-9582-8

Robert Hale Limited
Clerkenwell House
Clerkenwell Green
London EC1R 0HT

www.halebooks.com

Typeset by
Derek Doyle & Associates, Shaw Heath
Printed and bound in Great Britain by
CPI Antony Rowe, Chippenham and Eastbourne

PROLOGUE

Northern Texas, July, 1878

Ned Sloane reined in the horses as the Wells Fargo Concord reached a bend where the Red River forked left. Parkin, the guard riding shotgun, took up his Henry rifle and held it at the ready. The heavy coach's springs creaked as the team of six slowed and the stage yawed to the right.

A half-mile up the trail and on the other side of the bend, Sloane and Parkin saw six riders blocking their path. The stage drew nearer, and the Fargo men could see bandannas pulled over the riders' faces. Every man held a rifle to his shoulder, and all were pointed in the Concord's direction.

'Outlaws,' Parkin said.

Sloane snapped the reins and took out his whip. 'I'm gonna run through 'em,' he said. 'Start firing when you're in range.'

When the distance between coach and riders was around 300 yards, Parkin began shooting, levering the Henry rapidly as he directed fire at the men. The six parted, three reining their mounts to one side and three to the other. None of Parkin's shots found its mark.

As the Concord passed the riders, a man astride a roan gelding on Parkin's side fired his Winchester. The round caught the Fargo guard in the chest. He somersaulted, hitting the ground hard.

The rider who shot him, a tall man in black, swung his mount in behind the stagecoach. 'Get after it,' he shouted to the others. 'Shoot the driver and grab the reins.'

The men took off after the Concord and gained ground fast. As soon as he drew level the lead rider on Sloane's side began firing. Though his first shots only succeeded in splintering the coach's woodwork the rider stood in his stirrups and managed to steady his aim. His next bullet hit Sloane's temple and the driver crumpled with the reins in his hands.

A second rider was now level with the stagecoach on the other side. He stretched over, grabbed the side rail, and swung from his saddle into the driver's seat. He quickly grabbed the reins and heaved Sloane's body over the side. With the team of six horses still running at full pelt, he pulled back hard.

'Whoa!' he shouted. 'Whoa!'

The horses slowed, stopped, and the remaining riders caught up. They dismounted and the black-clad leader walked over to speak to the man who had stopped the coach. 'Any passengers, Jeb?' he asked.

The man called Jeb took off his bandanna and wiped sweat from his brow. 'Don't know, Everett. Saw nobody.'

Everett drew a Colt .45 from his holster. 'Anybody in there? Come out now, else I'll commence shooting.'

The Concord's springs creaked as someone within the coach got to his feet. A nervous-sounding voice answered: 'Please don't shoot, Mister. I'm not armed.'

'Come out where we can see you,' Everett said.

A slightly built man wearing a derby hat stepped cautiously from the coach. 'I'm the only passenger,' he said.

'Who're you?' Everett asked.

'Willis, sir. Hiram Willis.'

'What're you doing on the coach?' Everett asked.

'I'm an accountant with the Farmers' Mercantile Bank,' Willis replied. 'Being transferred from Dodge City to the Sweetwater branch here in Texas. In charge of some ledger books and account registers which are being transferred with me.'

Everett looked at the men around him. 'Accountant, huh? Say, fellas, we've got us the right man.'

The five others laughed and Everett levelled his pistol at Willis.

'Well, Mr Willis,' Everett said, 'I'd like you to point us in the direction of the *cash* being sent to the Sweetwater branch of Farmers' Mercantile. We ain't interested in no ledgers.'

Willis ran a finger under his collar and swallowed. 'There's a strongbox in the leather boot at the rear of the coach. But, like I said, it contains only ledger books and account registers.'

Anger flashed over Everett's face. He addressed a short, swarthy man nearest the rear of the coach: 'Toomey, unstrap that boot. Find the strongbox. Throw out anything that ain't it.'

Toomey unstrapped the leather cover at the

back of the coach, looked inside, and removed a padlocked metal chest. 'Just one thing in here, Everett; this box,' he said.

Everett cocked the hammer of his Colt. 'Throw it on the ground,' he ordered.

Toomey let the box drop. Everett walked over, took aim, and shot off the padlock. He motioned to Jeb. 'Quick – get it open. Let's see what's inside.'

Jeb hunkered down and threw open the lid. One side of the box contained a number of ledger books. Jeb took these out, grabbed each one by its cover, and vigorously shook the pages before throwing it down. At the other side of the box were rolls of parchment tied with red ribbon. Jeb tore the ribbons off these and unrolled the paper.

'You see, just as I told you,' Willis said. 'Account registers and ledger books.'

Everett wheeled around and put the point of his pistol to Willis's neck. 'Where's the money?'

All colour drained from Willis's face. 'W-What money?'

Everett hit Willis's ear with the butt of the gun. 'Don't play the dumb-ass with me, Mr Accountant. The cash being sent to Sweetwater to pay drovers' wages.'

Willis took a handkerchief from his pocket and used it to stanch the blood running from his ear. 'The cash for the Sweetwater branch was transferred yesterday by the Santa Fe railroad.'

Jeb walked over and grabbed Willis by his coat lapels. 'You lyin' little sonovabitch,' he said. 'I've watched them load the Sweetwater dough on to the Fargo Stage third Tuesday of every month since March.'

Willis put up his hands in supplication. 'You're correct, sir. You're correct,' he said. 'The change was agreed by the home office in Chicago only last month. It's just been put into practice.'

Everett again levelled his .45 at Willis and nodded towards Sloane and Parkin on the trail behind. 'Then why did these men take a run at us? Why not stop if they ain't carryin' cash?'

'Our contract stipulates Wells Fargo employees aren't to be aware what they carry on our behalf.'

Everett looked again at the coach and said, 'Toomey, check the boot under the driver's seat, then up top. Make sure there ain't nothing else.'

Toomey unstrapped the leather cover under the driver's seat and looked inside, then climbed on to the Concord's roof. After a minute he said, 'Nothing in front, Everett. Nothing up here either.'

Everett again pressed his pistol into Willis's

neck. 'That money being transferred by train,' he said. 'When's it taken out?'

'I believe the cattlemen's wages are being paid today,' Willis replied.

'Hell and damnation,' Everett cursed. 'They've even changed the payday.'

Willis's hands now shook visibly. He said, 'The cattle companies' arrangement with the bank is to draw cash and pay wages the day after the money arrives, sir. Now it's in the bank a day earlier—'

Everett cocked the .45 again. 'Willis, you've just outlived your usefulness.'

Willis began pleading. 'Oh, no, please – please. Don't kill me.' He paused, then added, 'I know something that might make up for your loss today.'

Everett's index finger began to squeeze the trigger. 'Know what?' he asked.

'Another money shipment. A big one. Leaves our Dodge city branch next Monday.'

'How much, and where's it headed?'

'I'll tell you, sir, I'll tell you,' Willis replied. 'If you'll promise not to shoot me.'

'OK, I won't shoot you,' Everett levered the hammer back. 'Now answer the question.'

'Fifty thousand dollars,' Willis said. 'It's going

to the Farmers' Mercantile branch in Buffalo Falls. Being sent out July twenty-second by the Santa Fe railroad. Arrives the morning of July twenty-fourth.'

'This Buffalo Falls,' Everett said. 'How far from here?'

'Two hundred miles south-west of Sweetwater,' Willis replied. 'It's over on the Western Trail.'

'And it'll definitely be there July twenty-fourth?'

'Yes, sir, it will,' Willis said. 'I'd stake my life on it.'

A tight smile played around the corners of Everett's mouth. 'Looks like you just did, Mr Willis. Shoot him, Jeb.'

Willis fell to his knees and wrung his hands. He looked up at Everett. 'No, no. I won't say anything, honestly. Please – you said you wouldn't shoot me.'

'That I did, Mr Willis. And I won't. Jeb will.'

'But—' Willis's cry was cut short as the cartridge in Jeb's Winchester ignited. The bullet smashed into the accountant's head and he spun to the ground.

Everett took the reins of his gelding. 'C'mon fellas,' he said. 'Mount up. We got some hard riding to do.'

1

Amos Kane and I had ridden hard since leaving Fort Larned. For over a hundred miles we followed the Arkansas River to Dodge City, looking for work, but no one was hiring. A trail boss in Dodge told us to strike out for Texas. 'Follow the Western Trail,' he said. 'Big herds being put together there for the drive north.' He reckoned we'd easily find droving jobs.

But by 1878 the railroads had pushed further south. Ten years earlier, Abilene in Kansas was where Chicago-bound cattle had been boarded. Now longhorns were taken on at railheads in any number of north Texas towns.

Could be droving work was harder to come by.

We figured that if that were true we might try ranching. A lot of new cattle outfits were being put together, and Texas covered a fair bit of territory.

Trouble was, we'd no cowpunching experience. For the last ten years we'd been cavalrymen, Amos a sergeant and me a corporal. Both of us signed with the Seventh in '68, just as the big Indian nations were pushed off their lands.

Amos and I, I'm glad to say, just missed General Hancock's unnecessary battles with the Cheyenne. A peaceful settlement with the Cheyenne and Lakota Sioux was still being negotiated when Hancock ordered an Indian village to be burnt to the ground.

Then all hell broke loose. The two of us were posted to Fort Larned in the aftermath, but still had a whole lot of mopping up to do. The Indian wars simmered for another ten years – and Amos and I got our 'baptism of fire' in skirmishes with the most dangerous tribes on the Plains.

You get to know a man's character in such situations. Amos was cool-headed, slow to anger and had a quiet way with him. Many thought his unruffled approach suggested a lack of mettle; some found to their cost that this just wasn't so. A fella who learned the hard way was Fort Larned's Indian agent, a big Irishman called Sturgeon.

One day we got back from a patrol and saw him

cuff a squaw with a papoose on her back. The blow caused the squaw to stagger and started the baby howling. 'Get along, damn you, red-nigger bitch,' he said to the woman.

Amos dismounted and went over to the agent. 'Sturgeon,' he said, 'here's no call to treat a woman that way.'

Sturgeon turned and shrugged dismissively. 'Woman is it, Sergeant? I see no woman. Just a red-nigger bitch who keeps pesterin' me for milk.'

'That's a baby on her back, Sturgeon,' Amos said. 'And from what I've seen of the meagre rations you're handing out, it's no wonder she's asking for more.'

'Ain't no business of yours, soldier,' Sturgeon answered. 'Now get going 'fore I knock you on to your blue-britched arse.'

The calm expression on Amos's face remained. He pointed to the store behind Sturgeon and said, 'I want you to go in there and get the woman a cup of milk.'

The Irishman looked at Amos as if he'd taken leave of his senses. 'Is it an eejit you are?' he said. 'I'll no' tell ye again – bugger off or I'll gie ye the hidin' o' your life.'

In one rapid movement Amos swung left and

drove his right fist into Sturgeon's gut. The blow caused the burly man to fold and, as he did so, Amos followed up with a left hook that caught his nose hard; it cracked loudly and blood started pouring down Sturgeon's shirtfront. Next, Amos took his army Colt from his holster and used the butt to club the Indian agent's jaw. This blow was the clincher; Sturgeon moaned and held up his hands. 'Enough, Jeesus, enough,' he said, sputtering. 'You're gonna kill me.'

'Next time I see you abusing any of these people, Sturgeon, I might just do that. Now, go inside and get this woman a cup of milk.'

Sturgeon rose with difficulty and went into the store. He came out a minute later with a cup of milk, and gave it to the woman. He stayed out of Amos's way after that, and I never heard tell of an Indian who suffered at his hands again.

In 1878 Fort Larned closed down. Most tribes had by then settled in the new Indian Territory south of Kansas, and the fort was surplus to the government's requirements. As ten-year men, the army offered Amos and me the choice of signing on again and taking a posting further east, or retiring on six weeks' pay. Like me, Amos had grown tired of endless patrols and of military life in general. We opted to stick together, take the money, and start afresh as civilians.

Which was the reason we went to Dodge in search of work. And why, three weeks later, we crossed into Texas to seek a new beginning.

2

The trail had been tough on us and the horses. Charley, my sorrel gelding, was noticeably thinner; I think he'd shed twenty pounds. Amos's paint didn't look much better. Amos and I vowed that at the next town we'd find a livery stable and give the animals a feed and rest. We reckoned we needed a meal and a bath, too – somewhere to shake off the dirt accumulated in the ten days since Dodge.

A little after noon we crested a ridge and saw a town on the far side of the plain. We rode the horses gently downhill and joined the rough road that wound towards it. At the side of the road, a half-mile out, a board nailed to a post told us the place was called Buffalo Falls. We got nearer, and could see the town wasn't particularly big: only three streets north to south, seven east to west. A railroad spur ran parallel with the easternmost edge, which was two blocks from Main Street.

The Houston Hotel and saloon took pride of place halfway down Main Street. A general store occupied most of the next block, and a hostler with livery stable was located at the far end. Amos and I left the horses, then walked back and went into the Houston saloon.

It took a minute for our eyes to adjust to the oil lamps after hours in the sun. As we went over to the mahogany bar a portly man standing at the far end nodded to us. Amos and I nodded back.

The barman said, 'What can I get you, fellas?'

'Two beers, thanks,' Amos replied.

As the barman poured the beers Amos and I looked on appreciatively and licked our lips in anticipation.

'Hot, isn't it, gentlemen?' The portly man had moved along the bar and now stood beside Amos.

'Sure is,' Amos said.

The man held out his hand. 'Allow me to introduce myself. My name's Walter Breen. Owner of the Houston Hotel.'

Amos shook his hand. 'Pleased to make your acquaintance, Mr Breen. Name's Amos Kane. This here's my friend, Luke Fisher.'

Breen shook my hand. 'You've both ridden far?'

'About eighty miles today,' I replied. 'Don't know how far altogether. Been in the saddle ten days since leaving Dodge City.'

'I hope you don't mind my asking,' Breen said, 'but are you in Buffalo Falls on business?'

Amos caught my nod and replied for both of us. 'Don't mind at all,' he said. 'Luke and me need work. Trail boss in Dodge told us we might find cattle-herding jobs on the Western Trail.'

'Ah,' Breen said, 'I'm sorry, Mr Kane. I don't think you'll find droving work here. Buffalo Falls is a railroad spur now. Southern outfits bring cattle here for shipment to Dodge and Abilene. End of a three-hundred mile drive. Drovers get paid, stay a few days, then start back again.'

Amos took a long draught of his beer, then wiped his mouth with the back of his hand. 'Yeah, Luke and I'd heard that,' he said. 'Reckon we'll rest a spell and head further south.'

'I hope you'll pardon a further impertinence,' Breen said. 'I notice you and Mr Fisher have a military bearing. You wouldn't by chance have been in the army?'

Amos grinned. 'That obvious, huh? Yeah, Luke and I just finished a ten-year stint at Fort Larned.

Getting used to being civilians.'

'Ah, yes,' Breen said, 'I read in the *Examiner* they were closing the Fort.' He took a cigar case from his pocket. 'Will you have cigar? Mr Kane, Mr Fisher?' We both declined but thanked him. He took one himself, bit off the end, lit it and drew in the smoke.

He exhaled, then said, 'Would you consider other work besides cattle-driving?'

'What kind of work?' Amos replied.

'I'd like to make you both a proposition that I think might be of interest,' he said. 'But it's a town matter and I'd like to do so in the presence of my colleagues. Like me, they're members of the town citizens' committee.'

Breen called to the barman, 'Elias, please give Mr Kane and Mr Fisher another drink. On the house.' He turned back to face us. 'Will you meet us in my office in thirty minutes?' He pointed to a door beyond where he had stood when we first came in. 'Through there,' he said, 'left at the end of the hallway.'

'We three head the citizens' committee. You've met Breen, of course.' The man speaking nodded at the two men seated next to him. 'Peabody here runs the feed and grain. McLehose owns the café and general store. I'm Abe Thoroughgood, I manage the Farmers' Mercantile Bank.'

Thoroughgood was a distinguished-looking man with thinning hair. Peabody was the youngest of the group, with pale skin and a wispy moustache. McLehose was heavy-set and had a weathered complexion.

Breen nodded towards a fourth man, the oldest in the room. He sat at the end of the table and had grey hair and a beard. 'Don't forget Sam,' he said. 'Sam Cole. He's our current town marshal. Wants to retire.'

Cole took a pipe from his pocket, which he started to fill. 'Got me a little house a block down from Main Street, Mr Kane,' he said. 'Wife's been naggin' me to fix it up for a while.' He lit the pipe and began puffing. 'I'm fifty-nine now. Some o' those whippersnapper herders are a mite difficult to handle on weekends. This job needs new blood.'

Amos shot me a quick glance and addressed Cole. 'Don't you have a deputy marshal?'

'Had me one, Tom Quincy,' Cole replied. 'Been writin' to his sweetheart back East for the past year. Left last week to go see her; thinking on gettin' hitched, I believe.'

Thoroughgood said, 'So you see, Mr Kane,

Buffalo Falls needs a new town marshal. Someone like yourself. Experienced in firearms and . . . well, not to put too fine a point on it, someone not afraid to deal with violent men. We believe you fit these requirements. Will you take the position?'

'You'd need a deputy, too,' said Amos.

'I explained that you were both looking for a job,' said Breen. 'We'd be happy to make Mr Fisher your deputy.'

'How much would you pay?' Amos said.

'A dollar a day and found for each of you,' Breen said. 'You'd room free here at the hotel. Mr McElhose would provide your meals. He'd bring them to you at your office.'

'We'd need autonomy,' Amos said.

'What's that?' asked Breen.

'The right to make rules people'll comply with.'

'I still don't understand,' Breen said.

Amos looked at Sam Cole. 'Mr Cole, you said you'd a problem with cowhands at weekends. You mean in saloons?'

'Yeah, hotels and bars, mostly. Sometimes in the street,' Cole answered.

'These cowhands, they armed?' Amos asked.

Cole puffed at his pipe but it had gone out. He

put it back in his pocket. 'Yeah, most of 'em got pistols.'

'The town needs a statute,' Amos said. 'Anyone entering leaves their guns at the marshal's office.'

'Wouldn't be popular,' Cole said. 'Drovers don't like to be parted from their sidearms.'

'If Luke and me take the job, we wouldn't be courtin' popularity, Mr Cole. We'd need that statute. Men liquored up are easier to handle when they can't draw a weapon.'

'I agree,' Thoroughgood said. 'On my last trip to Dodge I observed they work such a system. It would help make Buffalo Falls more civilized.'

Breen nodded. 'Makes sense. OK, Mr Kane, we agree. Statute's in place as of today. So, you'll take the job?'

Amos said, 'I'm willin'.' He turned to me. 'You, Luke?'

'Sure thing,' I replied.

Breen stood up. 'Then it's agreed,' he said. We all shook hands, then Breen turned to Cole. 'Sam, will you take Mr Kane and Mr Fisher over to your office and show them the ropes?'

Cole nodded. 'Be glad to,' he said.

Cole showed us the marshal's office, which was a block along from the Houston on the other side of the street. The following day we patrolled with him, visiting bars on Buffalo Falls' three main streets and the seven that intersected. There were few customers, though. Cole told us we'd arrived during a quiet spell.

Most customers at the places we went to worked at various town trades: carpenters, shopkeepers, gunsmiths and the like. Cole said there was a big cattle outfit due in town next week. Amos and I knew the drovers would be armed, so we rode out to the marker posts at either end of the town and put up notices about the new statute. This clearly stated that weapons had to be deposited at the marshal's office on entering Buffalo Falls. Failure to comply meant arrest and a spell in our jail.

The Thursday following our appointment, Amos and I placed chairs on the boardwalk in front of the office, and in the early afternoon saw a group of men ride into town. The lead rider was a tall man with black coat and hat. Judging by the way the other men deferred to him, he looked like their boss. What mostly caught our attention was that the men didn't stop when they drew level with us, but carried on to the Houston Hotel.

This they shouldn't have done: for each man carried a rifle in his saddle scabbard, and a sidearm in his gunbelt.

3

Amos stood up. 'We'd better have a word with those fellas,' he said.

I adjusted my gunbelt and picked up my Sharps '59. 'Yeah, I think we'd better,' I replied.

We crossed the street and began walking down the boardwalk opposite. As we neared the Houston Hotel we saw the men dismount and go inside, with the exception of one man, who walked toward McLehose's store. He was almost at the store when another man, a 'breed who portered for McLehose, came out with a box, intent on loading it on to a buckboard outside.

As the 'breed emerged he forced the man walking to pull up momentarily and give way. Simple courtesy didn't sit well with the man. He appeared to regard the 'breed as inferior, someone who should have backed into the store and out of is path.

'Out my way, you idle piece of horse-shit,' he said. He took his gun from his holster and begun pistol-whipping the 'breed, who dropped the box and raised his arms in an attempt to ward off the blows.

Amos levelled his Winchester at the 'breed's attacker. 'Stop that right now, mister,' he said. 'Else I'll be compelled to shoot you.'

The man glanced around and shot Amos a hostile look. He let go of the 'breed, then turned around and faced Amos. 'Who are you? he said.

'Town marshal,' Amos replied. 'This here's my deputy. Put down that gun. You're under arrest on charges of assault and disobeying the statute on carrying firearms.'

The man still had his pistol in his hand. He waved it towards the 'breed. 'This bum deliberately bumped me. I was givin' him a lesson in manners.'

'You're the one who needs a lesson in manners, mister. We saw what happened. The man didn't bump you.'

The man began to bring up his pistol. 'So you're callin' me a liar?'

Amos cocked his Winchester. 'I said drop that

pistol, mister.'

The man continued to bring up the gun. There was a sharp crack as the Winchester fired and the bullet tore the gun from the man's hand. He now lay writhing on the boardwalk and bleeding from the wrist.

'You bastard,' he said, 'I was gonna drop my gun. There was no need to shoot.'

'I told you twice to drop the gun,' Amos said. 'You didn't.'

I had positioned myself on the street beside the boardwalk and to the rear of Amos. I saw movement to my left and turned and raised the Sharps. At the hotel entrance, the man who Amos and I guessed was the group's leader stepped out.

He was tall, square jawed and wore a pencil moustache. The four other men stood behind him.

'What's going on here?' he said.

Amos stepped off the boardwalk level with me. He stood where he could cover both the man on the boardwalk and the men at the Houston.

'I'm Amos Kane, town marshal. This here's my deputy, Luke Fisher.' Amos nodded to the man he'd just disarmed. 'This man with you?' he asked.

'Yes, Mr Toomey's with me,' the leader replied.

'What's he done wrong? Why'd you shoot him?'

'First thing,' Amos replied, 'you men are all contravening a town statute. The notice you passed on the way into town states all firearms are to be handed in on arrival. Second, Mr Toomey here just assaulted a citizen. He also refused to put down his gun when I asked him to.'

'Didn't assault anyone, Everett,' Toomey said. 'Just had a run-in with a 'breed who bumped into me comin' out the store.'

Everett snorted. 'A half-breed? You shot my friend because he knocked into a half-breed?'

'Not quite,' Amos said. He pointed to the porter, who now stood back from Toomey at the entrance to the store. 'This man works for Mr McElhose, the store's owner. He came out carrying a box just as Toomey went in. Your man took umbrage at having to give way and pistol-whipped him. I shot him because he wouldn't lay down his weapon.'

Everett gave Toomey a sidelong glance, then studied Amos for a long moment. 'And you're going to arrest him?' he said.

Amos held Everett's stare. 'That's correct,' he said. 'He'll spend two days in the hoosegow. Be a ten-dollar fine for the assault.'

A man with a thin scar on his right cheek who

was standing alongside Everett moved forward. His right hand brushed his holster. Everett raised his arm and stopped him. 'Hold it, Jeb,' he said. 'Marshal Kane's got a point. Toomey should've gave way.'

He paused, then addressed Amos. 'Sorry, Mr Kane,' he said. 'We've ridden hard for two days. The men and myself are a bit trail-weary. Tell the truth, don't think any of us seen the notice.' He gestured with his thumb to the Houston's entrance. 'Just booked us into the hotel. Freshen up and a rest. I reckon Toomey's tiredness made him a bit fractious. You're right, he shouldn't a done what he did. I'll pay his fine and he can be your guest for two days. Me and my men will come with you now and check in our weapons.'

'Be obliged if you would,' Amos said. He motioned with the Winchester to Toomey, who now stood rubbing his wrist. 'Marshal's office is over there on the left, Mr Toomey.'

I picked up Toomey's pistol and we walked to the office with him in front, followed by Everett, Jeb and the others. Amos and I brought up the rear.

While I put Toomey in a cell at the back, Amos took possession of the men's arms. On my return Everett took a billfold from his pocket and paid

Toomey's fine. 'Name's Everett Stark, Mr Kane,' he said. He nodded to the man with the scar. 'This here's my brother, Jeb. We're on our way south. Friend of mine told us about some big spreads for sale near the Gulf Coast. We plan to buy one, start a ranching outfit. We'll rest up a while. Booked at the Houston till Tuesday.'

Amos wrote a receipt for the ten dollars. 'Sounds like a good business plan,' he said. 'I hope it works out OK. Call into the office when you're leaving, I'll hand your weapons back then. Mr Toomey will be free to go on Saturday.'

A few minutes after the Starks left Amos said, 'Look like ranchers to you?'

'They don't,' I replied. 'More at ease totin' a gun than ropin' a steer, I reckon.'

'My thoughts exactly,' Amos replied.

'That Jeb fella was about to pull his pistol before Everett stopped him.'

'Yeah, I seen that,' Amos replied. 'Everett was weighing somethin' up. Five of 'em might've outgunned us, they'd a mind to.'

'Might've.'

We were interrupted by a knock at the door.

'Come in,' Amos said.

The 'breed porter from McLehose's store

entered. He held his hat between his hands and nodded deferentially at Amos.

'Come to say thanks,' he said. '*Hombre* you arrest beat me with gun. You stop him. I very grateful.'

'You're more'n welcome,' Amos said. 'Your attacker's gonna spend a couple of days with us.' Amos opened the desk drawer and took out the ten dollars that Everett had paid for Toomey's fine. 'You still hurtin'?' he asked.

'No, *mi amigo*,' the 'breed replied. 'Most hits from pistol on my arms. They strong from carrying boxes.'

Amos gave him the ten-dollar bill. 'Here, take this,' he said. 'It'll help compensate.'

The 'breed looked amazed. 'Really, *mi amigo*? Is OK to take? Comp. . . ?' He scratched his head. 'I not know this word.'

'Compensate,' Amos replied. 'Means we make him pay for attacking you.'

'You good man, *mi amigo. Muchas gracias,* Mr – what your name?'

'Amos Kane,' Amos replied. 'This here's Luke Fisher. You?'

'My name Sugarfoot.'

'Sugarfoot?' Amos smiled. 'How'd you come by a handle like that?'

'Be long story. Take time to tell,' Sugarfoot said.

'Take a seat,' Amos said, pointing to the chair beside the desk. 'Tell your story. Luke and I ain't in a hurry.'

'I Cherokee, born in Toosaw reservation in Kansas,' he said. 'My father part Spanish, part Indian. My mother full-blood Cherokee. When I a boy, ten, eleven years old, I like to climb a mesa near our reservation. It very steep, not many places to grip for hands or feet. I become good climber. My people give me Cherokee name: means "sure of foot". Later – I seventeen – become tracker, work for Army at Fort Dodge. Soldiers ask me to say my name in English. I tell them. They laugh, call me "Sugarfoot", say it kick-name.'

'Nickname,' Amos said. 'What outfit did you track for?'

'Yes,' Sugarfoot said. 'Nickname, that the word, Mr Kane. I tracked for Captain Freemont, '69 till '72. General Sheridan come then, he bring his own trackers. I go back to reservation. Army later move Cherokees. I come to Buffalo Falls three years since, work with Mr McLehose.'

'Luke and I were Army, too,' Amos said. 'Fort Larned. Only just retired.'

'I think you soldiers when I first see you,' Sugarfoot said. 'Now you lawmen. I sure you do good job. Wish you much luck.' Sugarfoot got up, walked to the door, and nodded to us. 'And again, *gracias, mi amigos,*' he said. 'My father dead, but my mother stay on reservation in Indian Territory.' He held up the ten-dollar bill. 'I send this to her.'

Sugarfoot said *adios* and, as he opened the door, another visitor came into the office.

It was an exceptionally pretty young woman.

4

'My name's Sophia McLehose. My father's quite busy and couldn't manage over. He asked me to bring lunch for both of you and the man in custody.' Sophia was in her early twenties, with long blonde hair that framed her face and spilled on to her shoulders. She smiled at Amos. 'You're Mr Kane?'

'That's correct, ma'am, Amos Kane. 'This here's my—'

Sophia interrupted, 'I know, your deputy Luke Fisher. My father gave me your names before I left.'

She placed a basket covered with a gingham cloth on the table. 'Lamb fries, beans and potatoes. With some fresh-baked bread. I do hope you enjoy it. Not much choice at the café today, I'm afraid.'

Amos and I both shook her hand. 'Please to meet you, ma'am, and thanks very much for bringing the vittles,' I said. 'I'm sure they'll be fine'.

'Sophia. Please, call me Sophia.'

She removed the gingham cloth from the basket and took out two plates, each of which was wrapped in a separate cloth to keep the meal hot. We watched as she removed these and set two steaming plates on the table. 'Better eat before it gets cold, gentlemen,' she said. She lifted bread and a third plate from the basket. 'This one's for your guest; shall I take it to him?'

'No thanks, Sophia,' Amos replied. 'I'll take it through in a minute.'

Sophia nodded, picked up the empty basket, and went to the door. 'Well, it's really nice to meet you. Oh, by the way, Father wants me ask you both to dinner on Saturday. Will you come?'

'You'll be there?' Amos asked.

Sophia gave Amos a coquettish look. 'Of course,' she replied.

'Then we'd be delighted.'

At noon on Saturday we went to release Toomey. When Amos unlocked his cell, however, he still sat on the cot, rubbing his wrist. I'd bandaged the wound when we'd taken him into custody two days before. The .45 slug had creased the skin just below his thumb, but I could see it would heal quickly.

'You're free to go, Toomey,' Amos said.

The man stood up and glared at Amos. 'Still say you'd no right to go shootin' me.'

'Just a flesh wound; it'll heal soon.'

'Ain't talkin' about the wound,' Toomey replied. 'Talkin' about your right to shoot me in the first place.'

'Toomey,' Amos said, 'we've been over this. If you'd dropped your pistol when I asked, you wouldn't have been shot.'

'Well, this ain't over,' Toomey replied. 'You got the drop on me Thursday. Won't get the same chance next time.'

'Will there be a next time, Toomey?' Amos replied. 'You makin' a threat?'

I gave Toomey his hat. He looked at Amos and shrugged. 'Just sayin',' he replied.

'Well, Toomey, I was you I would say no more,' Amos said. 'We can always extend our hospitality a bit longer.'

Toomey grunted, shuffled to the door and banged it as he went out.

'Idle threat?' I said.

'Ain't so sure,' Amos replied. 'Don't like him or the bunch he runs with. You and I gotta start watchin' our backs.'

'Oh, Father, not that Indian story again,' Sophia McLehose said. Amos and I and she and her father were seated at a big oak table in the house above their store. We'd eaten a substantial dinner and were now on the coffee.

'But it's a true story, sweetheart,' McLehose said. 'It's how Buffalo Falls got its name.'

'My father gives too much credence to old Indian tales, gentlemen,' Sophia said. 'I think it's something made up to tell round the campfire.'

'It's OK, Sophia, I'd love to hear it,' Amos said. 'Please go ahead, Mr McElhose.'

'Did you notice the big bluff on the left as you entered town?' McLehose said.

'You mean the hill with the cliff at one end?'

'That's the one,' McLehose replied. 'Story goes that before the Spanish introduced horses to America in the sixteenth century, Indian tribes in this area hunted on foot. Buffalo meat was their staple. Only plentiful, though, when the herds migrated south.

'At those times the entire tribe would chase the buffalo for miles towards the bluff. Once there they had willow branches, rocks and such placed to corral them – force them in either side – and drive 'em up the slope. Once at the top, of course, the stampedin' herd had nowhere to go but down. Legends say it looked like a great cascade pourin' over the side. Hence the name – Buffalo Falls.'

'Smart Indians,' I said.

'Surely were,' said McLehose. He drained the remainder of his coffee and put the china cup back on its saucer. 'Makes you realize how far this country's come in a couple of centuries. Heck, when Martha – God bless her soul – and I came here ten years go this town was nothing more than a collection of shacks. Now we got indoor plumbing, telegraph communication and a railroad.'

'Mrs McLehose is no longer living?' Amos asked.

'No, she died from consumption seven years ago,' McLehose replied. 'The first three years were hard. Reckon it took a toll on her health.'

Sophia got up and began clearing the plates. 'Come on, Father, let's not get maudlin. I'll take these dishes to the kitchen. Why not take your guests through to the sitting room and give them a drink?'

After she'd left the room, McLehose said, 'She don't like me talkin' about her mother. Only fifteen when Martha died. She took it hard.'

He shook his head and stood up. 'But she's right of course, I'm not mindin' my manners,' he said. 'Please, come through to the sitting room and I'll get you both a drink.'

In the sitting room McLehose invited Amos and me to sit, then gave us both a glass. A selection of liquors in cut-glass decanters stood on a silver tray atop an engraved rosewood table. McLehose tapped the top of each decanter. 'Brandy, bourbon, sherry – ah, yes.' He selected one from the back of the tray. 'I think you'll both like this. It's Scotch whisky, gentlemen, but not any old brand. This is something special, a twelve-year-old single malt.'

He poured a generous measure into each of our glasses. Amos took a sip first and I followed. I felt a pleasant warmth as the potent liquor hit my innards. It was smooth to the taste, too; a lot less harsh than the spirits I was used to.

'What do you think?' McLehose asked.

'Good,' I replied. 'Very good.'

'Mr Kane?'

'Best I've had.'

Sophia came into the room and her father gave

her a glass. 'Your usual sherry, sweetheart?' he said.

Sophia nodded. Her father filled the glass and she took a sip. 'I meant to tell you, Father,' she said, 'there's a group of men in town, ranchers. I spoke to the gentleman managing the outfit, a Mr Stark. He tells me they're headed to the Gulf Coast, they intend buying a ranch there. I thought I'd give them an introduction to Uncle Phillip.'

Sophia turned to us and said, 'I'm sorry, Mr Kane, Mr Fisher. I know it's rude. But I've just returned from paying my uncle a visit; he's a property agent in San Antonio. I only now remembered something that might be beneficial to his business. I intended to mention it to my father earlier.'

'This man, he's looking to buy in San Antonio?' McLehose said.

'He said the Gulf Coast area. Uncle Phillip deals with property in that part of the state.'

'You're right, my dear, indeed he does,' McLehose replied. 'And you gave him one of Phillip's business cards?'

'Yes,' Sophia replied. 'Mr Stark seemed a genuine fellow. I'm sure he'll get in touch when he gets there.'

Amos and I exchanged glances but said nothing. A half-hour later we thanked the McLehoses, took our leave, and began walking back to the office in the middle of a thunderstorm.

The dim lamp lights at either side of Main Street gave scant illumination. We reached the end of the block opposite the office and stepped into the street, intending to cross.

A moment later a shot rang out. The bullet hit a post on our left and ricocheted into the boardwalk.

5

A second shot followed immediately; this time the slug kicked up a spout of muddy rain water at Amos's feet. The flash from the muzzle came from the alleyway opposite. We drew our pistols and dashed across to take up positions at the corners of the blocks on either side.

'Only one shooter,' Amos said.

'Yeah, I think so,' I replied. 'Don't know if he's still there.'

There was the sound of a garbage can being knocked over at the back of the building. Amos and I sprinted up the alleyway and rounded the corner. There had been a little light on Main Street, but at the back it was coal-black. A flash of lightning illuminated the alley briefly, but we saw no one. We stood for a moment, but heard nothing more.

'Can't see nobody,' I said. 'Reckon he's gone.'

'Must've followed us since we left the McLehoses. These back yards run parallel with Main Street.'

'Just as well the light ain't good,' I said. 'Been daylight he might've found his target.'

'I agree,' Amos said. 'Can only be one party behind it, though. C'mon, let's get back to the Houston.'

Though the Stark outfit and Amos and I all boarded at the Houston, in the two days since he arrived we hadn't seen the would-be rancher or any of his men, with the exception of Toomey. This was because when Toomey was in custody one of us would remain at the office while the other undertook patrolling duty. In the early hours, with patrols done, Amos and I took turns on alternate nights to go to our rooms and get some proper shut-eye.

Now that Toomey had been freed Amos and I closed the office when we finished our first patrol. Tonight that had been at nine, before we went to the McLehoses.

On arriving at the Houston we ran into Breen, who was sitting in the foyer smoking one of his cigars. 'Evenin' Marshal, Deputy,' he said. 'You're both in early tonight. It's only gone midnight. Town's a bit quiet this weekend, guess it's the weather.'

Amos looked at me and raised an eyebrow. He turned to Breen. 'Wouldn't exactly say that,' he said. 'Mr Stark and his men, they in the bar?'

'No Marshal, 'fraid they're not. Did you want to see them?'

'What time they get in?'

'Early evening I think, four or five. Same since they booked in. They have dinner around seven, go to the bar and order a few drinks, play a hand of poker. Go upstairs around eleven.'

'All of them retire that time tonight?' Amos asked.

'Yes, I think so. I've just come from the bar. Only people there are Elias my barman, and two drummers from Abilene.'

'Did you see Toomey, the man we released today?'

'Little swarthy fella?'

'The same,' Amos replied.

'Yes, he was there. Went upstairs same time as the others.' Breen gave Amos a quizzical look. 'Anything wrong, Marshal?'

'No, I don't think so,' Amos replied. 'Just checking something. Thanks, Mr Breen.'

*

Next day Amos and I took breakfast as usual at the office. Afterwards we decided to exercise the horses. We rode out for five miles to the far side of the plain where we'd first sighted the town. There we followed a narrow valley, above which the land rose beside a thick stand of cottonwoods. We rode off trail and up until we gained the crest of the hill, then reined in the horses. In the valley below a group of riders come into view. They were headed in the direction of Buffalo Falls.

Amos took his Bullock's binoculars and thumbed the wheel until he gained focus. 'Stark and his men,' he said. 'They've an unusual interest in the lie of the land up here for men who intend travellin' south.'

Amos and I had discussed the shooting the night before, but I brought it up again. 'The thing that still stumps me is where they got the gun,' I said. 'We took all their arms on Thursday.'

'Been thinkin' on that some more,' said Amos. 'What if they didn't miss the sign coming into town? Guessed maybe there was a fair chance they'd have to check in their weapons. Why not cache a pistol or two out here?'

'It's a possibility.'

'As I mentioned last night,' Amos continued, 'Toomey's most likely to be the shooter, yet it could be any one of 'em. We saw nobody, got us no evidence.'

'We know the Starks are up to *something* though.'

'That they are,' Amos replied. 'And after what happened last night, they might think it better if we weren't around to stop them.'

On our patrols Amos and I had stopped by all the bars in town. Most were simply drinking dens: a bar, a sawdust floor and a scattering of tables where customers played faro, poker and the like. The Alamo saloon on Sixth Street was different.

There was the usual long bar and tables for gambling. But at one end there was a raised stage with a piano, where saloon girls got up and performed a nightly song-and-dance routine. The women wore low-cut dresses and kicked up their heels to reveal shapely ankles beneath their flouncy petticoats. When the stage show was done, though, the girls provided another kind of entertainment in the rooms upstairs.

The first time Amos and I visited we were greeted by two such 'sporting gals': a dark-haired beauty called Michelle and a petite blonde called Rosamund.

Had they been dressed differently, and in another setting, neither woman's 'profession' might have been guessed; both possessed real elegant looks. Michelle, who was French, took a particular shine to me. She walked over right off and introduced herself.

'Hello, *mon cher,*' she said. 'You're the new lawman, is that not so? My name is Michelle.'

'Deputy marshal, ma'am, yes,' I replied. I pointed to Amos. 'This here's my friend. He's the actual town marshal.'

'But you are the good-looking one, *oui*?' Michelle said. She took a hold of my shoulders and kissed my cheek. I smelled her perfume and felt her firm breasts press into me. A second or two went by, but she clung tighter still. It had an effect; I felt something stir south of my gunbelt.

The other girl, Rosamund, went up to Amos and tickled his chin. 'Oh, I wouldn't say that,' she said, 'The marshal ain't bad-looking, either.'

'What is your name, *mon cher*?' Michelle asked me.

We introduced ourselves. At that moment, however, a man got on the stage and began to play the piano.

'We 'ave to go, Luke,' Michelle said to me, pointing to the stage. 'Our routine begins, you understand? Promise you'll come back to see me. Please, *mon cher*?'

I was quite taken with Michelle, and a little lost for words.

She gave me a pleading look. 'Promise?'

I cleared my throat. 'Promise.'

At the office, later that Sunday, Amos and I had got back from the first of our evening patrols. The town was still quiet and I decided to go to the Alamo and pay Michelle a visit.

An hour later she and I had finished making love and we lay on our backs in a brass-postered bed. Michelle said, 'You like, *mon cher*?'

'Very much.'

'You not with a woman for a long time, I think.'

'No, not for a while.'

'Your friend the marshal, he likes my friend, Rosamund?'

'I'm sure he does.'

'She ask me to ask you. She tells me she like to see him.'

'I'll mention it to Amos.'

'You will, *mon cher*? He visit her, it make her very happy.'

'I will.'

Michelle kissed me again and caressed my cheek. 'You think me a bad woman, Luke?'

I pushed a stray hair from her face. 'No, Michelle, I don't.'

'You not think, I take money, that why I like you?' She paused, 'Is not true.'

I smiled. 'It ain't?'

'Women here only think of dollars when they lie with men. I do with others, Luke, but not with you. I like you, *mon cher.* I like you very much.'

Her face took on a worried look. 'You and Marshal Kane should take care here in Buffalo Falls. Bad men in town, I think they want to hurt you.'

'What makes you say that, Michelle?'

'Last night two men come into the Alamo,' she said. 'Both tall like you.' She pointed to her cheek. 'One 'ave scar here. They sit at table near the stage, and I hear them speak. Man with the scar look very angry, he say to other man, "We better take care of the marshal and his deputy before Wednesday." Toby – he play the piano – start music then. We 'ave to give show, I hear no more.' The worried look still clouded her face. 'These words, "take care", mean they want to do bad thing, is not so?'

'The other man, was he wearing black?'

'*Oui.* Black coat, black hat. Is true, they want to harm you and Amos?'

'We had a run-in with them last week, jailed one of their men. Reckon they were still angry. Don't mean anything.'

'But you *will* take care, *mon cher*?'

'I will, Michelle, I promise.'

I left the Alamo a half-hour later, a little after ten. I cut through to Main Street and was almost opposite McLehose's when I saw a man and a woman in front of the store. The woman opened the door and light flooded the boardwalk. It was Sophia McLehose and Everett Stark. At that moment Stark said something and Sophia laughed. He kissed her on the cheek then, and said goodnight.

Back in the office I told Amos what I'd just witnessed. 'Yeah, remember, he told her he's looking for a ranch near the Gulf Coast. She's got an uncle there who's a property agent,' he said.

'Thought you'd be more disappointed at Stark and her being so friendly.'

'You mean Sophia getting close to Stark tonight?'

'Yeah; the other day it seemed you'd taken

quite a shine to her.'

Amos laughed, 'Yes, got to admit I had.' He shook his head. 'Hell, Stark though? Just can't figure a woman. . . .'

'Well, speaking of figures, you got a well-built admirer at the Alamo who's anxious to see you.'

'Rosamund? Thought she was just being friendly.'

'Probably. But some of those sportin' gal's get to have their favourites.'

'Don't see as I could be hers. Ain't paid her a visit.'

'Yet.'

Amos grinned. 'Yet,' he said.

I remembered then what Michelle had told me, and told Amos what she'd overheard.

'Confirms it was one of them shooting last night,' he said. 'Also confirms what I said about them being up to something. I'm sure there's something fishy about their story about being ranchers.'

'Well, we won't have to wait long to find out. They're supposed to be headin' south on Tuesday. They gotta drop by and pick up their weapons. I think you and I should tail 'em for a while, see where they go.'

6

The Starks dropped by little after six on Tuesday morning. Amos and I had only arrived moments before, and I was putting coffee on the stove. The door swung open and Everett walked in, followed by his brother Jeb. Toomey and the three other men waited outside.

Everett tipped a forefinger to his hat. 'Mornin' Marshal, Deputy,' he said. 'Nice day for a ride, ain't it? Might cover a hundred miles or more before sundown.'

Amos took the rifles and pistols from the gun safe and handed them over. He gave the Starks the shells separately, wrapped in old newspaper. 'Took the liberty of unloading all your weapons,' he said. 'Wait till you're clear of town before you load them again.'

Jeb took the shells and sneered. 'What's the matter, Marshal? Think we're gonna shoot up the town before we leave?'

Amos looked straight at Jeb and held his gaze. 'Maybe. Thought I'd remove the temptation, in any case. Like I said, don't load up till you're clear of town limits.'

The Starks went to the door, and Everett turned around. 'Don't worry, Marshal, we'll do like you say: we ain't looking for trouble.' He made a little waving motion with his Colt and gave a wry smile. 'Gotta mention, though – if trouble finds us, we'll be more than happy to deal with it.'

We let fifteen minutes go by before riding after them. Their newly made tracks were easily visible on the trail south, which wound through a series of low hills. Stark and his men came into view after four miles, at a place where the hills ended and the trail struck out across a semi-desert, almost to the horizon.

We stopped and Amos focused his binoculars. 'They're still riding south,' he said. 'Got to be about five or six miles ahead of us.'

'Think they can see us from there?'

'Only if they look back,' Amos replied. 'And only if they've got glasses.'

He thumbed the focusing-wheel again. 'I don't

think we need ride further, Luke. I may be wrong, but I think the trail south picks up again between those two buttes. This track seems headed in that direction. They're almost there and they ain't deviating.'

He handed me the glasses and I saw the two distant buttes. Sure enough, the six riders were headed straight between them. 'You're right, Amos,' I said. 'It does look like they're headed south.'

'Nothing to stop them turning a bit further on, of course. But they've got to have ridden south for eight or nine miles now. If they'd planned coming back for any reason, I'd expect them to have changed direction before this.'

We rode back to town and had been in the office less than an hour when Sam Cole knocked and came in. He had a piece of paper in his hand and looked a bit unsettled. 'Telegram for you, Amos,' he said. 'Sorry, Willie Knox at the cable office brought it to me by mistake. Seems to forget I ain't marshal any more. Apologies again, I couldn't help but see what it says.'

Amos took the telegram and read it, then passed it to me. It told of the hold-up of the Wells Fargo stage near Sweetwater, where the coach had been headed one week before. No money had been carried, but the driver and shotgun guard were killed, together with an accountant working for the Farmers' Mercantile Bank on his way to the Sweetwater branch. The telegram also said the county sheriff had picked up the tracks of six riders. These were thought to lead in the direction of the Western Trail.

'This Sweetwater, Sam, how far is it from here?'

'About two hundred miles north-east.'

Amos turned to me. 'The Starks and their men,' he said, 'they got here on Thursday, two days after the Sweetwater killings.'

'Too much of a coincidence?' I replied.

'It is. The Fargo stage was headed for the Farmers' Mercantile Bank in Sweetwater, and we got a branch of the same bank here in Buffalo Falls.'

Amos crossed to the window and looked down the street. 'Sam,' he asked, 'do you know when money's delivered to the bank this month?'

'No I don't, Amos,' Cole replied. 'They keep changing the cash transfer dates, to deter hold-ups. This month's shipment might already be here.'

'Doesn't the bank want the marshal there when the money arrives, in case of trouble?'

'Tom and I used to attend when the money

came by coach,' Cole replied. 'Only the Fargo driver and his guard were with the stage then. Now the money comes by train. The Wells Fargo company have their own railroad car. Thoroughgood meets the train with a wagon, and he and the Fargo men take the cash to the bank.'

'Thanks, Sam,' Amos said. 'I think we better have a word with Abe Thoroughgood.'

'The only people with knowledge of tomorrow's cash transfer is myself and the accountant's office in Dodge,' Abe Thoroughgood said. Amos and I were standing in his office at the Farmers' Mercantile Bank soon after our talk with Sam Cole. Thoroughgood was seated on the other side of an oak desk inlaid with green leather.

He pointed to a large metal safe on his left. It was solid-looking, made of forged steel with lettering that said it was manufactured by the Burke & Barnes Safe Company of Pittsburgh. 'Normally we hold enough cash to keep us going for a month or so. But we've got a big cattle outfit coming in tomorrow and another two early next month. The cattle outfits need the cash to pay drovers' wages. So tomorrow's shipment is an unusually large amount.'

'How much?' Amos asked.

'Fifty thousand dollars.'

Amos gave a low whistle. 'That *is* a large amount.'

'There should be nothing to worry about, Mr Kane. The cash is always escorted by four armed Wells Fargo men.' Thoroughgood paused and shook his head. 'Do you really suspect Mr Stark and his men for the Sweetwater hold-up? I was told they'd ridden south. They were thinking of buying a ranch somewhere near the Gulf of Mexico.'

'Yes I do. I think the rancher story's a bluff. It's quite a coincidence they show up here six days before the money's due.'

'But didn't you say you and Mr Fisher followed them out of town?'

'We did, but I now think that's part of the bluff. After reading this telegram, I'm sure they're the ones who held up the stage last week. I've a hunch they'll swing around at some point and head back.'

'You may well be right, Mr Kane, but I say again, these cash transfers are sent at irregular intervals. No one but myself and the people in the Dodge office know that money's on the train.'

'The bank accountant who got shot at Sweetwater, would he know?' Amos asked.

Thoroughgood looked a bit nonplussed. 'Yes – yes, I suppose he would. But why would he reveal that to his attackers?'

'He was the only passenger, Mr Thoroughgood,' Amos replied. 'I think it likely Stark and his men killed the guard and driver before they shot the accountant.'

'Meaning?' Thoroughgood asked.

'Meaning he might have told them about tomorrow's shipment, in exchange for his life.'

'But they killed him.'

'He might have thought they wouldn't kill him. Desperate men do desperate things, particularly when their life is threatened. I think the Starks held up the stage thinking it had money. When they found it didn't, they'd have been angry. The accountant could've told them about the shipment as a way to survive.'

'Yes, I can see that,' Thoroughgood said. 'Well, the train's due at noon tomorrow. What do we do?'

'The railroad car Wells Fargo use, does it have protection?' Amos asked.

'Yes,' Thoroughgood replied. 'The walls and door are steel-lined to withstand dynamite. And it can only be opened from the inside. Why do you ask?'

'I'm calculating the odds of the Starks succeeding if they hit the train before it gets to town. If the railroad car is as secure as you say, they're more likely to pull a robbery here, when the door is opened.'

'Do you think there's a real likelihood of them trying to stop the train before it arrives?'

'Like I say,' Amos replied, 'just calculating the odds. They'd gain easier access when the train stops. On the other hand they'll have more opposition: Luke and me and Sam Cole, not forgetting the Fargo men. If they hit it before, their efforts'll be for nothing if they can't get into the car.'

'Bit of a quandary,' Thoroughgood said.

'Yeah, it is. Other way is Luke and I, with Sam's help, go and escort the train. But from how far out? They could hit it anywhere.'

'Well, Mr Kane, it's your decision. What do you think?'

'The train's least vulnerable while it's moving. If it *is* stopped, the car's security might prevent it being breached. The transfer point here is the weakest. I think we should stay, cover the Fargo men while the money's brought to the bank.' Amos turned to me. 'What do you say, Luke?'

'A bit six of one, half a dozen of the other,

Amos,' I replied. 'But yes, I think the town's the weak spot.'

'Then it's agreed. We'll be waiting when the train gets in at noon tomorrow.'

7

On the far side of the plain the hills shimmered in the midday heat. The railroad tracks ran in a straight line towards them and, even with binoculars, we strained to see the place where their perspective diminished. All of us were anxious for first sight of locomotive smoke or the sound of the train whistle.

Buffalo Falls station was shaded by a timber roof and was deserted except for the three of us: me, Sam Cole and Amos. We'd taken positions just after sunup – Cole at the the platform's south end near a water barrel; Amos at the north end close to a privy; and me crouched on a section of roof above the platform's edge. For hours we'd kept a watch in all directions for riders, too: whichever way the Starks had chosen to ride in from, we had it covered.

But now it was almost twelve, and we'd seen neither riders nor train. Noon came and passed and we began to grow impatient. After what seemed an age, Amos called over and asked Sam the time. Cole took his watch from his vest. 'Twenty past,' he said. 'Never usually more than fifteen minutes late.'

Another ten minutes went by, then we heard the faint sound of the train's whistle. Amos looked through his binoculars. 'It's coming,' he confirmed. The whistle continued to sound until the train drew into the station.

On its approach, the conductor leaned from one the rear carriages and waved a red flag, then the locomotive shunted to a stop and emitted a great blast of steam.

The conductor jumped off and ran towards us. He was red in the face and looked extremely agitated. 'Train's been robbed,' he said. 'Six men. Dry-gulched us on Pine Ridge gradient. Three Fargo guards shot dead. One's badly wounded – I've stopped the bleeding, but he needs a doctor.'

Sam turned to Amos and me. 'Pine Ridge,' he said, 'it's about fifteen miles from here. Track winds around a series of hills, Pine Ridge is the steepest. Loco can only take it at ten miles an hour.'

'Got a litter on board?' Amos asked the conductor.

'Yes,' the conductor replied. 'There's one in the back car.'

'Go get it. Luke and I will carry the Fargo man to McLehose's store. It's only a short distance from here.' Then to Cole he said, 'Will you get the doc, Sam? Bring him to McLehose's?

'Sure thing, Amos.'

'I don't think the bullet's hit any vital organs,' Doc Taylor said. 'It's in the upper intestinal tract. Missed the aorta, liver and right kidney.' The Wells Fargo guard was lying on a cot in the store room at the back of McLehose's store. Amos and I and McLehose and his daughter were in the room with Taylor and the injured guard. Sam Cole left after bringing Taylor and went to talk to the conductor and driver.

The Wells Fargo man had been drifting in and out of consciousness when Amos and I carried him to the store. Sophia had bought hot water and clean towels and had been mopping the man's brow when Doc Taylor arrived.

The injured man gave a groan and showed signs of coming to. 'The bleeding's been stanched,' Taylor said. 'Shock and infection are the main dangers now. I'd like to give him some laudanum to help the shock. It'll also keep him sedated. Then I'll anaesthetize him and remove the bullet. After that . . .' he paused, 'he's young. With luck he might recover.'

He opened his medical bag. 'Oh, blast,' he said, 'I don't have any laudanum with me. Sophia, would you please go to my office and bring it? It's in the cabinet on the left, next to my desk. The office is open.'

Sophia put down the towel she'd been using to mop the guard's brow. 'Right away, Doctor Taylor,' she replied, then left.

The guard groaned again and opened his eyes. 'Where am I?' he said.

'You're in Buffalo Falls,' Taylor replied. 'I'm a doctor. You've been shot in the stomach. I'm going to give you something to help the pain, then I'll remove the bullet.'

The Wells Fargo guard looked over and saw Amos and me. 'You're the marshals who brought me here?' he asked.

Amos nodded. 'Yes, we are,' he replied. 'Doc here thinks you're gonna be OK.'

Doc Taylor said, 'It's best you don't talk now, save your strength.'

'No, it's OK,' the guard replied. 'I want to tell

the marshals what happened.'

'OK,' Taylor said. 'But you won't be able to talk for long. I'm going to give you some medicine. It'll make you sleepy.'

The guard moved slightly and winced. 'The gang stuffed kerosene rags in the car's air vents,' he said. 'Set them alight. In a few minutes there was nothing but thick, black smoke in there. None of us could breathe. They were intent on smoking us out the minute the train stopped. We *had* to unlock the door. Our lungs were fit to bust for lack of air.'

'Did you see any of them?' Amos asked.

'Yes,' the man replied. 'Two big men, one with a scar. Didn't get to see any others. We'd no chance to sight our rifles when we got the door open – they commenced shooting straight off. Killed three of us, left me for dead. Nothin' else to call it but mur—'

His voice trailed off. His eyes closed and he lost consciousness.

'It's shock,' Taylor said.

At that moment Sophia re-entered the room and gave the laudanum to the doc. 'I think I'll administer chloroform first and remove the bullet,' Taylor said. 'I'd be grateful if you'd leave me to it, gentlemen. Sophia, I'd appreciate if you'd stay and help with the dressings.'

We left the store with McLehose and stood on the boardwalk. Amos said, 'Mr McLehose, could you give Luke and me provisions to cover a few days' ride? We're going after the men who did this.'

'Sure, Mr Kane,' McLehose replied. 'I'll put together some supplies.'

'One other thing, Mr McLehose. I'd like the help of your porter. He's an experienced tracker.'

'Sugarfoot?' McLehose replied. 'He's out delivering to a customer, shouldn't be long. I'll tell him. When are you leaving?'

'As soon as we can,'Amos replied.

We went back to the station where we found Sam Cole. While we were at McLehose's he'd spoken to both conductor and engineer. 'The engineer wasn't aware of anything until a rider came up and got into the front with him and the fireman,' he said. 'Aimed a pistol at the man's heart, told him to stop the train and stay put. Both he and the firemen did as they were told.

'Conductor got out to see what was happening. Was told to stay inside, too, else get shot. Only a few passengers on the train. They and the railroad people heard men get on the roof, then saw black smoke and heard shots fired. After that the gang rode off with the dough. Conductor says the whole thing took less than ten minutes.'

'That's helpful,' Amos said. 'It backs up what the Fargo man told us. The guard also identified Jeb and Everett Stark, so we know for sure who was behind the robbery.' Amos took off his hat and wiped the sweat band. 'Sam, could you take care of business for a few days? Luke and I are going after them. We're taking McLehose's porter with us. He's an ex-army tracker.'

Cole scratched his beard. 'Only three of you, Amos? Wouldn't you be better scarin' up a posse? There's six of them, remember. Killed three at Sweetwater, now another three at Pine Ridge.'

'Luke and I have faced worse odds, Sam. 'Sides, a posse would take too long to put together. Likely most men we'd get would have little experience. Could slow us down. No, we've a better chance if we leave now and catch them before they put any distance between us.'

'Well, I'm more'n happy to put on my badge again and take care of the office till you get back. Tell the truth, I've been gettin' under my wife's feet. By the way, I spoke to Abe Thoroughgood. There's a five-thousand-dollar reward for recovery of the money.'

8

The three of us reached Pine Ridge just after two o'clock and Amos and I dismounted. Sugarfoot walked his pinto back and forth, taking signs from the thick scrub surrounding the track. There was still a strong stench of kerosene at the spot where the train had been forced to stop.

After a couple of minutes Sugarfoot pointed east. 'All men ride that way,' he said. 'Six horses, two heavier than others. Make deeper mark in ground.'

'Some of that'll be the money,' Amos said.

'Any idea how much fifty thousand weighs?' I asked.

'Never thought to ask Thoroughgood. Depends on the dollar value of the bills. If it was to pay wages, I'd guess mainly tens, fives and ones.

I think maybe twenty pounds or less.'

'Think they've spread the weight over two horses?'

'Maybe not. They're most probably using two big geldings to tote most of the weight. I think one of them'll be carrying the money. The other, maybe supplies. Could be they're intent on a long ride.'

The two of us mounted up. Amos walked his paint over to where the tracker stood. 'What do you think, Sugarfoot? Can you track them?'

'All land flat from here to Indian Territory,' he replied. 'Easy ground to take sign. If they keep going this way, I think they headed to Red River. After that Comanche, Kiowa, Apache country.'

'The Indian Nations harbour any number of lawbreakers,' I said. 'A lot of places for them to hide. Might not be easy to find if we don't catch up.'

'Yeah, they got an advantage if they know where they're headed,' Amos replied. 'But we got an advantage, too. We got a good tracker, and they can't be more than three hours ahead.'

We got going and rode until the sun began to set. The land we covered was mainly mixed-grass prairie, spread under a wide sky that stretched right across the horizon. Late in the afternoon a bald eagle flew low near us, and a young white-tailed deer that might have been its prey ran from the grama grass and took shelter in some scrub. Soon afterward we found a stream next to a grove of piñon trees and made camp for the night.

With the horses hobbled, we lit a fire and set up the Dutch oven. We cooked a pemmican beef stew and had coffee on the boil when Sugarfoot rose suddenly. 'Hear riders,' he said. Amos and I stopped what we were doing, took our rifles, and walked beyond the piñons to where we'd a view of the prairie. It was almost completely dark but we were able to make out two riders heading in our direction. They slowed when they saw us and reined their mounts to a standstill.

We could just make out the lead rider, who wore a duster coat and a hat with a feather sticking out of the band. 'Hope you don't mind, mister,' he said. 'We're a bit dragged out. Saw your fire and thought we'd come over and ask if we could mooch a cup of coffee.'

We kept our rifles at the ready and Amos said, 'Come closer. We can't see you.'

The riders walked their horses nearer until we saw them clearly in the light of the fire. They were both around sixty years old. The man who had spoken had a white beard and was quite fleshy.

His companion was almost the opposite; rail-thin with a drawn face and a walrus moustache.

'Don't blame you bein' cautious,' the bearded man said. 'Seth and I just came from the Injun Nations. Fair number of characters on the shoot there, gotta keep your wits close and your six-guns closer.'

'OK, come on in,' Amos said. 'Take a seat by the fire. Coffee's on, won't be a minute.'

The riders dismounted, and the bearded man extended his hand. 'Name's Partridge,' he said. 'Reuben Partridge, this here's my pard, Seth Tolleson. We do a little pannin' on the Canadian, sometimes the Red River. When we don't find gold, we skin beaver, sell the pelts in Abilene and Fort Worth. When we've gold, we sell it anywhere we find a buyer.'

Amos said, 'Amos Kane.' He nodded to me and Sugarfoot. 'Luke Fisher. The other man's travelling with us.'

I poured fresh coffee into five tin mugs and passed them round. 'You cross the Red River today?' I asked Partridge.

'Yes, crossed by ferry late this afternoon,' Partridge replied. 'Tar Creek, near the state boundary.'

'Pass any riders?' Amos asked.

'Saw nobody since we crossed the state line.' He nodded to Sugarfoot. 'Ain't that man a tracker? Hope you don't mind my nose, but are you men pursuing somebody?'

'Yeah,' Amos replied. 'We're marshals. Hunting six men who robbed the cash box from a train bound for Buffalo Falls.'

'Train robbers?' Partridge said. 'Darnation, would you believe it? They kill anyone?'

'Three Wells Fargo men, left one for dead. Same gang shot and killed three more near Sweetwater last week.'

'Well, don't that beat all?' Partridge shook his head. 'What the hell's this country coming to?' He swallowed some coffee and wiped his mouth with the back of his hand. 'They must've crossed Red River before we got to Tar Creek. We was pannin' a mile or two up river before we came over.'

Partridge took a twig from the side of the fire and pointed east. 'Tell you this, Mr Kane, they're headed the right way. Once they reach the Nations, you'll have the devil's own work rooting 'em out if they go to the mountains. A lot of folks think Injun Territory's flat, but it ain't. There's Wichita Mountains this side and the Windin' Stair range further east. Plenty of spaces to go to ground. Harder to track, too.'

'How far the other side of the Red River before you reach the mountains?' Amos asked.

'About seventy miles to Wichita Maountains,' Partridge replied. 'How much of a lead they got?'

'They'd have had to camp for the night same as us,' Amos replied. 'About three or four hours.'

'Well, it's a two-hour ride from here to the ferry,' Partridge said,. 'Once you get into the Nations you might gain ground. Easier if you could get some local help.'

Tolleson hadn't got a word in while Partridge had been talking. He cleared his throat then and said, 'What about Aitcheson?'

Partridge looked at Tolleson. 'Of course, Seth!' he exclaimed. 'Why didn't I think of that? Aitcheson, he'd know about strangers passing through. Seth's talking about the old Scottish Comanche agent at Doyle's Bend, Mr Kane. Your robbers would have to go through Comanche land first, and no one passes without Aitcheson knowin' when they come, and where they're headed. He's real close to the chiefs. They're his eyes and ears.'

He drew three parallel lines in the ground with the twig, each a foot apart. He indicated the left line. 'We're here,' he said. He pointed then to the centre and right lines. 'This here in the middle's the Red River, this line on the right's the Comanche reservation.' He drew a fourth line at right-angles through the centre of all three lines. 'Your robbers would have to cross the river, as we did, at Tar Creek. From there it's only five miles to Comanche land. Your tracker will find their trail easy enough. If they're headed to the Wichita range, it'll go north-east before Doyle's Bend, which lies south of the mountains, about eighty miles into Comanche land. If they go that way and get to the mountains first, might be hard for your man to track them. Only thing to do if their trail does deviate is to go on and speak to Aitcheson. His Comanches will know exactly where they are, even in the mountains.'

'This Aitcheson, you're sure he'll help us?' Amos asked.

'Just mention my name. Ben Aitcheson owes Seth and me some favours.'

The next morning we rose at sunup. Partridge and Tolleson had shared our camp for the night, and the five of us breakfasted early. Before we went our separate ways we thanked the men for their help; they in turn thanked us for our hospitality and wished us good luck.

When we reached the Red River it was still quite early. The ferry was on other bank, where the ferryman sat smoking a clay pipe. The man was bald and had a ruddy complexion. He looked up and saw us, raised his hand in acknowledgement, and set to work with the ropes.

He reached our side and secured the raft. 'Ten cents apiece, gents,' he said. 'That includes the horses.' We paid him and led the horses on to the raft. My gelding became skittish and began nickering. I shielded his eyes with my coat and got him quieted down. Amos's paint and Sugarfoot's pinto went aboard without protest; both stood quietly, quite unaffected by the creaking timbers and the water rushing around us.

'We're following six men who crossed late yesterday,' Amos said to the ferryman. 'Happen to see where they went?'

The man paled a little. 'Sure, I saw them. Arrived here a little after eight. I was on the other side securing the ropes for the night. Got a cabin a little ways off. Told them I was done for the day, said they'd need to wait till morning. One of them says, "We're in a hurry, got to cross now." I repeat I'm closed for the day, tell them to come back tomorrow. He takes a rifle, aims it right at me. Says, "Bring the ferry over now, mister, else you'll not see tomorrow." Tell the truth, I feared for my life. Told them I'd comply, unhitched the raft and took 'em across.'

'What did they look like?' I asked.

'Two big guys leading them. One with a scar, he was the man who threatened me. Four other fellas about average build.'

'Did you see which way they went?' Amos repeated.

'Yes I did. Six of them all rode east, headed to the Comanche Nation.'

9

We'd ridden for about twenty miles when Sugarfoot found where the Starks had camped the previous night. We dismounted and followed him to a hollow where there were signs of a recent fire. We could see the grass had been flattened where bedrolls had lain.

Sugarfoot took a stick and poked the ashes. He ran his fingers through fine ash near the centre. 'Still warm,' he said. 'Fire last used two, three hours ago.'

'They must have started out later than us,' I said.

'I think so,' Amos said. 'Means we've narrowed the gap. I'd say they've a twenty-mile lead.'

'How far to Doyle's Bend?' I asked.

'We've ridden for three hours since Red River.

I'd say about sixty miles from here. If their trail keeps going east, it's likely they're riding further into the Nations.'

'If they keep going, they'll be headed for Arkansas.'

'Or they could swing south, back into Texas. Still hot for them there, though. They'll know the county sheriff's busy circulatin' their descriptions. They'll also know we're not far behind, maybe with a posse. Which means the further they ride, the more chance of us catching up.'

'Which leaves. . . ?'

'Leaves the mountains. What Partridge said, I figure that's the most likely. They'll want to go to ground. Lie low somewhere until the heat's off.'

We mounted up and rode on. The landscape in the Comanche Nation was similar to what we'd already crossed on both sides of the Red River: mostly flat with occasional low hills. The grasses were much the same as on the Texas plains, too: mostly grama, with stretches of sand reed and switchgrass. The horses had a particular liking for blue stem, which looked a bit like wheat and grew almost everywhere.

They cropped the blue stem enthusiastically when we stopped for a breather at streams, where we also filled our canteens. These grasses were useful in another way, in that they grew at least a foot high. This made it easy for us to follow the tracks made by Stark and his men, which so far had continued east without deviation.

Five hours after we discovered the spot where the Starks had camped the flat plain ended and the landscape changed. The vegetation was now scrublike and there were more trees: mainly piñon, cottonwoods and shinnery oak. The trail wound through these trees and rose gradually to the crest of a hill, where we saw a range of mountains about five miles to the north-east. Minutes later we reached a fork where a side trail headed off in the direction of the mountain foothills. The main trail continued east towards Doyle's Bend.

Sugarfoot indicated the left fork. 'Men go that way,' he said. He spurred his pinto and came to a piñon tree, where he dismounted and began to study the branches overhanging the trail. He looked at one branch in particular for a minute, then motioned to Amos and me. 'When men pass they break this,' he said. He took his finger and touched where the the branch had sheared. 'Sap of piñon still sticky. Take only two hours to harden. Riders no more than that time ahead.'

Amos examined the branch, then took out his binoculars and studied the trail ahead. 'If they're two hours ahead they are certainly beyond those foothills now.' He gave the glasses to me. 'Look at the area where this trail comes out, just in front of that peak.'

I took the glasses, focused, and followed the contours of the trail. It declined gradually for a mile or two from where we were, then dipped further to a dried-out arroyo. From there it snaked upwards for another two miles to the area below the peak Amos had mentioned. The ground there was composed entirely of shale and fragmented rock.

'I see what you mean.' I handed the glasses to our tracker. 'The ground changes up ahead, Sugarfoot,' I said. 'Here, take a look and see for yourself.'

Sugarfoot studied the trail below, then brought the binoculars up to see where it came out. He held focus a while longer, then frowned and gave me the glasses. 'Bad ground. Be difficult to track.'

'Then I think it's best we do what Partridge suggested,' Amos said. 'Ride on to Doyle's Bend and speak to Aitcheson.'

Doyle's Bend Indian camp was situated on an open stretch of land on a fork of the Wichita River. On approach we could see that the community comprised a hundred or more tepees and timber huts. The Indians who watched our approach were mainly squaws and children, their curiosity aroused by the strangers in their midst. As we rode further into the camp a number of young boys ran alongside us, laughing and whooping and waving little coup sticks.

Beyond the first cluster of dwellings we saw a substantial-looking log cabin, which we took to belong to Aitcheson. We were headed towards it when five young Comanche men came out and ran towards us, gesticulating menacingly. They were almost upon us when Amos and I reached for our pistols.

'Don't touch those guns, lads!' The man who had spoken had come out of the cabin behind the Indians and was now standing on the stoop. He looked to be about seventy, and had leathery skin and a goatee beard. He wore a US Army forage cap, but the rest of his dress was civilian. There was a Henry rifle in his hands, which he had pointed at us.

He said something in Comanche to the Indians and they stood to one side. He made a little waving motion with barrel of the Henry. 'What's your business?'

'We're marshals from Buffalo Falls, Texas,'

Amos replied. 'Chasing a group of men who robbed a train there and stole fifty thousand dollars. Are you Mr Aitcheson?'

'Indeed I am, lad. But I'd like ye to explain why that brings you here. This is a Comanche reservation.' He paused. 'And how do ye know my name?'

'We got it from someone who knows you, Reuben Partridge. He told us you may be able to help.'

'You know Reuben?'

'We camped with him last night at Red River. He said to mention his name.'

Aitcheson grinned and put down the Henry. 'Oh he did, did he, the auld reprobate? OK then, come away in.'

He spoke to the Indians again in their native tongue and they dispersed. We dismounted, tied the horses to the hitching post and followed him. We introduced ourselves and Aitcheson took a pot from the stove and handed us cups. 'You've got to excuse the Indian lads giving ye a rough reception, Mr Kane. You see, they're no' keen on strangers. And I don't like them to think they're in any danger, either. That's why I told ye no' to go for your guns.'

He poured coffee into the the cups and

continued, 'We had that bother when Black Horse left the reservation last year. The battle of Staked Plains – you might have heard of it?'

'Yes,' Amos said. 'Luke and I are ex-army. Served at Fort Larned.'

'Then you'll know it's sometimes hard to keep the peace. The chiefs here are settled OK. But I've had to earn their trust, and do my best to look after their interests. Don't want any more trouble breakin' out.'

'I understand,' Amos said. 'We'd like to get our job done and be off Indian lands as soon as we can. We figure the men we're pursuing might have a hideout somewhere in the mountains. Sugarfoot here has followed their trail, leastways till eight miles back. There's a track there that splits off in the direction of the mountains; they're headed that way.'

'I see. I now know why you came to see me, Mr Kane,' Aitcheson said, 'The ground's mainly shale.' He looked at Sugarfoot and gave him a sympathetic nod. 'Awfy hard ground to track, son.'

'Partridge told us the Comanches have a knowledge of the mountains. Might know where their hideout is.'

'Oh, there's no doubt about that, Mr Kane.

They know every inch of the Wichita range. Tell you what – it's near dark now. There's a wee hut out back where the three of you can bide the night. I'll have a word with the chiefs first thing in the morning, You can get under way then.'

'That's very kind of you, Mr Aitcheson,' Amos said. 'We'd very much appreciate your hospitality.'

At six the next morning we were ready to strike camp when Aitcheson came over to us. 'Everything all right, lads?' he asked. He nodded to his cabin. 'Coffee on the stove, bacon and beans nearly ready, too. If you'd care for some breakfast?'

'That's kind of you, Mr Aitcheson,' Amos replied. 'But we've already breakfasted, thank you. We'd really like to get going.'

'Aye, you're right, Mr Kane. Ye'll no' rest proper until these men are dealt with. Well, as promised, I spoke to the chiefs. I said they'd know where your outlaws are, and they do. You said you knew the name of the outlaw's leader?'

'Stark,' Amos replied.

'Aye, Stark. The Comanches have watched him and his cronies comin' and goin' in the mountains for a year or more. He's built a cabin at the far end of a canyon the Indians call Coyote Tail. You enter the canyon through a narrow pass. You'll recognize the entrance: there's two pillars of rock about fifty feet high; they stand either side. The pass is narrow, mind – barely enough room for a man on a horse.'

Aitcheson handed Amos a rough map drawn in pencil. 'See, you'll no' need to backtrack, either. The entrance to the canyon is only five miles' straight ride north of here. When you get near the mountains, you canna miss the two pillars.' He took a pencil from behind his ear and indicated the spot. 'Just here, you'll see them as clear as day.'

'This place where Stark has a cabin, is it far from the other side of the pass?' Amos asked.

'The chiefs tell me the canyon is shaped like a V and is completely enclosed, and trees cover most of the canyon floor. The pass leads you into the wide end. Stark's cabin is up at the narrow end, next to the canyon wall, two or three miles.'

'I don't know how to thank you, Mr Aitcheson, Amos said. 'I doubt if we could've located them, but for your help.'

'Any thanks are due to the Comanches, Mr Kane, they know their land,' Aitcheson said, then shook our hands. 'Best of luck, lads.' He tapped the side of his nose. 'And take care. That Stark sounds a nasty bugger.'

10

After a short ride we saw the Wichita range ahead. There were few gaps in the mountains facing us, which were fronted by a series of formidable bluffs stretching six miles from west to east. It was easy to spot the twin pillars; they looked like huge gateposts and were situated at a place where the bluffs recessed. It would have been hard to guess that this niche was actually the beginning of a pass to the canyon behind; from where we stood it looked like a dead end. It was only when you rode into what appeared to be the chamber's end that you saw that the recess turned sharply right . . . and realized it was the beginning of a route through.

We rode at walking pace, but in fact we couldn't have gone faster anyway. The trail twisted and turned tightly and allowed us only to proceed single file. After we had ridden for about fifteen minutes, the pass widened suddenly and ran straight for few hundred yards. We covered this ground quickly and came out where the high escarpments at either side of us widened further, and from this vantage point we could see the valley Aitcheson had described.

Coyote Tail canyon looked a giant amphitheatre; it was completely surrounded by cliffs, 200 feet or more high. We had emerged at the south end, above the canyon, which was a mile or so wide. The valley was thick with cottonwoods for three-quarters of its length. Three miles distant, at the north end, these trees gave way to a clearing, beyond which the ground rose again to the cliffs. As Aitcheson had explained, this was the narrowest point and was where the canyon ended.

The three of us took the binoculars in turn and surveyed the terrain, then Amos took his bandanna and wiped sweat from his brow. 'No wonder they chose this place,' he said. 'This passage is the only way in. They probably figured they were completely safe.'

'A secret valley known only to the Starks,' I said. 'And the Comanches.'

'They'll be aware the Indians know of it, that's for sure. But it's a hundred to one they'll figure a posse will never find it.'

'Might mean they're less likely to be on their guard?'

'Well, Aitcheson says their cabin's at the north end, though we can't see it from here. It's open ground there, though. They'll be foolish if they don't post a watch. It will allow them to see an approach.'

Sugarfoot pointed to where a rough track wound to the middle of cottonwoods below. 'Four riders go that way,' he said. 'Other two separate, one each side of canyon.'

'They've split their forces,' Amos said.

'Backs up what you said,' I replied. 'Stark must have posted two of his men near the top.'

'We should be OK through these trees, plenty of cover. Where they thin out, though, that's when they'll see us.'

We rode down the incline and joined the trail through the cottonwoods. A twenty-minute ride brought us almost to the north end of the tree line, where we dismounted and tethered the horses. If we'd ridden on into the clearing, we'd have known we'd be an easy target for anyone watching, so we took cover behind the last of the trees and scanned again with the binoculars.

Stark's cabin stood on a hill where the west and east bluffs met at the extreme edge of the clearing's north corner, a quarter-mile from where we were. The rear and sides of the cabin were snug to the cliff face, which meant any approach had to be frontal – and the cabin's two windows gave clear sight of any approach.

The bluffs to our right and left at this point were only 500 yards apart. Narrow ridges on either side were a good vantage point for any shooter.

'I'm convinced Stark will keep a couple of men on watch, one at either side of these bluffs,' Amos said.

'Yeah. If we were to go on we'd be in clear sight, from both sides and the cabin,' I replied.

'We could wait for nightfall, try then. It's a full moon this week, though. They'd have no trouble spotting us. The only thing in our favour so far is that they don't know we're here.'

At that moment there was a loud whinnying from one the horses. We ran back to where they were tethered in time to see an animal disappear into the scrub.

'It was Charley we heard,' I said. 'Coyote spooked him.'

'I spoke too soon,' Amos said. 'They'll know we're here now.'

Amos was proved correct, as seconds later we heard a rifle shot, rapidly followed by another. 'Signal shots,' he said. 'One either side. They're warning those in the cabin.'

I quieted Charley and the three of us went back to the edge of the clearing. Almost at once rifle fire tore into the trees near our position. One bullet stripped a branch on my left and another hit the brush a yard from where Sugarfoot stood.

'I don't think they can see us yet,' Amos said. 'But they're firing from the cabin and either side of the bluffs.'

'If one of us can hit the shooters either side of us,' I said, 'we can eliminate flanking fire.' I pointed to a covert of cottonwoods on our right, which stood out from the tree line and afforded a better view of the cliffs on both sides. 'I'll go to those trees and target the bluffs.'

'OK, Luke. Sugarfoot and I will cover you.'

As I sprinted over, the men on the bluffs saw me and began firing. Their bullets kicked up the earth around my heels. Amos and Sugarfoot couldn't offer cover in either direction as they didn't have the angle of fire from their position. When the four in the cabin began shooting at me, however, return fire from our side made sure their shots were wide of the mark.

I reached cover and turned my attention to the man on the east bluff. He was on a ridge roughly halfway up the cliff face behind a large boulder. He fired from either side of this rock, but every now and then he stood to take aim and I noticed he was exposed for longer.

Meanwhile the shooter on the west side had less of a target: the trees on his side of the covert obscured my position. He fired continuously anyway, but his bullets zinged harmlessly through the branches further back.

I sighted my Sharps and fired on the man on the east bluffs, reloading as fast as I could. One of my rounds chipped a piece off the rock, so I knew I had his range. He began to shoot over the top of the boulder more often, and when he did so he was vulnerable. I put in a fresh cartridge, pulled back the hammer, and aimed where his head had been moments before. A second later it bobbed up again and I squeezed the trigger. The round found its target and he fell back.

The man on the west bluff now fired into the trees near me. While Amos and Sugarfoot kept up fire at the cabin, I hotfooted over and took cover behind a tree on his side of the covert.

The shooter was shielded by a crevice on a ledge of rock, but was vulnerable when he stood out to take aim. He did this and got off a couple of quick shots that splintered a stump on my left. I flipped the Sharps' graduated gunsight and concentrated on his position. My first shot gave me his range and I adjusted the sight. He moved out and I fired again. The bullet caught his chest and he spun off the bluff and dropped to the canyon floor.

I went back to the tree line where the others were. Amos was reloading his Winchester while Sugarfoot continued shooting with his Henry.

'Good work,' Amos said. 'Glad to see your sharpshootin' skills are still intact.'

'Took me a while to get their range,' I said. 'But it's two less to worry about.'

Amos pointed to the cabin. 'This hideout presents a different problem, though. It's like a fort. Slam up against the bluffs, no way to work around it. And they've got a clear sight from every angle.'

While we talked, one of Sugarfoot's shots hit the bluff above the cabin and ricocheted upward. The round dislodged a smaller rock near the top of the cliffside and set a section of loose stones falling, several of which clattered on to the cabin roof.

'Some of the rocks above the cabin are quite loose,' Amos said. 'Pity we couldn't start a rock fall. Might flatten the cabin.'

One boulder at the very top of the cliff looked precarious and gave me an idea. I pointed to it and said, 'Be ideal if we could dislodge some of the shale beneath that big rock. If it fell it would take some loose stones with it. The cabin's right underneath.'

'OK,' Amos said. 'Let's try. Might get it to tumble.'

The three of us fired on the base of the rock for a couple of minutes, but to no effect; it refused to budge.

'Damn,' I said. 'If it had worked it might have done the trick.'

Sugarfoot nodded to the canyon behind us. 'I go climb mountain further back. They no see me there,' he said. 'Work my way round to top and push rock. Start fall. Men forced to leave cabin, you shoot or arrest them. Is good idea, *mi amigos*?'

'I saw those cliffs as we came in,' Amos said. 'The bluffs there are almost vertical. The only ledges are up this end, where the shooters were.'

'*Sí, mi amigo*, is true. But further back they not see me climb. Bluffs there are out of sight.'

'You're right, Sugarfoot, they are,' Amos

replied. 'But the sides are as smooth as a baby's backside. Didn't see cracks or suchlike for hand-holds.'

'My name Sure-of-foot for good reason, *mi amigo.* The bluffs I climb as a boy in Kansas, they same as here, like wall. I manage to get to top OK.'

Amos looked at me and I nodded my agreement. 'If you can make it, fine,' he said. 'But would you be able to shift that rock? It looks no lightweight.'

'I be porter, remember? Carry boxes all day. Don't worry, *mi amigo,* I strong, shift rock no problem.'

'OK, it's worth a try,' Amos said. 'When you're ready to move the rock, signal us.'

'I will. When rocks come down on men in cabin, I climb back down this end, be easier.'

'OK,' Amos said. 'But wait till we get all four of them first.'

The Starks and the two others stopped shooting shortly after Sugarfoot left. Amos took his glasses and trained them on the hideout. 'Saving their ammo till they can see us.' He focused on the area beside the cabin. 'They've got their horses corralled on the left and might run if Sugarfoot succeeds. It would be better if we were nearer, but we can get there quickly enough if they ain't shooting at us. Get ready to make a dash for the cabin the second they're distracted.'

11

Sugarfoot proved his climbing skills thirty minutes later when we saw him on the cliffs above the cabin. He moved quickly round to the rear of the rock and raised his arm to signal he was ready.

'Get ready, Luke,' Amos said, then moved out and raised his arm in reply. Shots from the cabin immediately ripped into the trees at either side, and Amos dodged back for cover.

Sugarfoot waved back in acknowledgement. We next saw him exert every effort to move the rock; he put his shoulder to it and his back arched as he strained to the task. Moments later we saw a wobble – the boulder had rocked slightly on its fulcrum. Sugarfoot heaved and again the rock shifted a little.

He retreated several paces then and ran at it,

using a combination of momentum and sheer strength to wrest the stone from its foundation. The boulder rocked once more, appeared to be suspended in mid air, then finally rolled over. It continued to roll and picked up pace, dislodging smaller rocks, which tumbled down the cliff in its wake.

The moment the landslide was under way, Amos and I could see that those in the cabin had heard the noise; the rifles aimed from the cabin's windows were withdrawn as the four inside realized the danger and scrambled to get out.

We ran when we saw this and had narrowed the distance to fifty yards when the door of the cabin burst open. The Starks made their exit with Toomey behind them, and seconds later the cabin collapsed. The fourth man failed to escape in time and perished in the debris.

The Starks and Toomey had saddlebags slung over their shoulders and made a dash for the corral. They saw us and fired while they ran, but their shots flew wide.

Amos and I dropped to a kneeling position and at that moment Toomey stopped and wheeled around. He managed to raise his rifle but got no further; a round from Amos's Winchester hit him and he reeled backwards.

Everett and Jeb glanced back and saw Toomey fall; they dropped to the ground and lay prone behind a slight rise. There was now only thirty feet between us.

'Everett, Jeb, drop your rifles and we'll take you back for trial,' Amos said. 'No one else needs to get shot.'

'Hell, yes, Kane,' Jeb said, 'we'll do just that. Die another day, eh? A necktie party in a few weeks or a shootout with you now. I know which I prefer. The one with better odds.'

I trained the Sharps on their position. The rise didn't afford them much cover, but then Amos and I were just as exposed. But to shoot, one of them would have to rise from the dip, which meant placing himself in a direct line of fire.

After what he'd just said, I guessed this would be Jeb. He lay on the right of the depression and I saw the top of his Stetson. I sighted the rifle and waited. I didn't wait long, for moments later he rolled to his left, jumped to his feet, brought his rifle to his shoulder and pulled the trigger. I followed his moves, raised the Sharps to where he stood, and fired. I got off my shot a fraction of a second ahead of his; my round caught his chest and he keeled over. His shot flew over my head.

Everett saw his brother die and raised his arm.

'Don't shoot, fellas,' he said. 'I give up.'

'Throw your rifle and sidearms over where we can see 'em,' Amos said. Everett complied and we told him to get to his feet.

'The money,' Amos asked, 'it's in those saddle-bags?'

'All fifty thousand,' Everett replied. He looked at Amos for a long moment. 'I'd like to make you boys a proposition. You're both ex-army, that right?'

'Right,' Amos replied.

'How long did you serve?

'Ten years, both of us.'

'Can't have been too generous a retirement pension. And your marshal's pay ain't much either, that right?'

'Right,' Amos replied.

'So why don't we split the money? Twenty-five grand for me, twenty-five for you. I go my way, you go yours. Nobody'd be the wiser.'

'We would,' Amos replied.

'Hell, c'mon, fellas. Don't make me beg. OK, split the dough three ways. Sixteen thousand and change for each of us.'

'Our army pay was earned one way, Stark,' Amos said. 'Same with anything we've made as marshals. Honestly. The money here ain't yours to take, ain't ours either. It belongs to the bank you stole it from, where it was headed when you killed three men to take it. It's goin' back to Buffalo Falls, and so are you.'

An hour later we'd saddled up for the ride back. Sugarfoot had descended the cliff and helped me cover the dead with shale rock. Amos, meanwhile, had cuffed Stark and used one of the dead men's horses for the saddlebags containing the money, and another for the supplies we carried.

When we'd finished placing stones on the last mound, I said to Amos, 'That should keep the buzzards off 'em. We ready to go?'

'Yeah,' he replied. 'We'll take the three spare horses with us and ride them in turn. Give the others a rest, help us get back quicker.'

'Might have to make camp before too long,' I said. 'Only a few hours before dark.'

'Yeah, been considerin' that,' Amos replied. 'Thought we'd clear the mountains and get halfway to Red River by nightfall.'

We made camp near the spot where we'd first sighted the Wichita range the day before. I got a fire going and put the Dutch oven on the heat. We had some salted beef left, and I made a stew to which we added bacon and beans. I set some coffee on the boil and dished out the stew.

Amos walked over to his paint and took his Winchester from the saddle scabbard. He placed the rifle near the fire and took out the keys to Stark's handcuffs.

'We're gonna eat,' he said to Stark. 'And I'm goin' to uncuff you. Any wrong moves and I'll shoot you, that clear?'

'Much good it would do me if I made a run for it,' Stark replied. 'This is Comanche country. I ain't no fool.'

'Maybe you ain't,' Amos said.

Everett took a slug of his coffee. 'Idea to kill them men at the train, wasn't mine.'

'Wasn't?' Amos replied.

'No, I told Jeb we could take the dough without shootin' anyone. Jeb paid me no heed. I'd no control over him.'

'Same with the Fargo men at Sweetwater?' I said. 'Jeb's idea to kill them, too?'

'It was,' Everett replied. 'I reckon if the bank gets their money back, I might serve some time, but I won't be guilty of murder.'

'There's something you mightn't know that could see a different outcome,' Amos said, 'if you're lying about Jeb being the only killer.'

Everett snorted sarcastically. 'Oh yeah, what's that?'

'One of the Fargo men you shot, he survived,' Amos replied.

12

Early next morning we had the horses saddled and were preparing to move off when we heard riders on the trail heading towards us. We mounted up just as a band of Indians came over a rise a half-mile from where we were. When they saw us they slowed to a trot, but continued to ride in our direction.

'Comanches,' Sugarfoot said. 'Be a hunting party, I think.'

They came nearer and we could see there were five of them. I guessed most were aged about twenty, but one man, who rode in front and whom I took to be their leader, was nearer forty. All five were naked to the waist and wore breech-clouts. The leader had a couple of eagle feathers stuck in his hair, which, like the others, he wore with a centre parting. Their hair was long and plaited, came over their shoulders and reached almost to their waists. Each Comanche carried a rifle, which he held at rest across his horse's neck.

'You speak Comanche, Sugarfoot?' Amos asked.

'A little, what I picked up when I was with Captain Freemont.'

'Good, we might need you to translate.'

The leader raised his right arm and said something in Comanche. Amos turned to Sugarfoot. 'You know what he said?'

'He talks about us trespassing, say this be Comanche land.'

'Tell him we're marshals returning to Texas,' Amos said. He nodded to Everett. 'And that we're taking this man back for trial for robbery and murder. Say we found him holed up in Coyote Tail canyon.'

The leader listened to what Sugarfoot said, then replied. This time he became quite animated, waving his arms as he spoke. When he'd finished, Sugarfoot said, 'I think he no like white men. He say he no care why you here. Tell me his Indian name is *Parrywahsaymer* – mean Ten Bears in English. He say he and his men are hunters, don't stay on the reservation at Doyle's Bend like others. White man steal Comanche land, he say, force his tribe from their northern territories. Treaties are dishonoured and what land white man give Comanche, he treat as his own. They don't have enough food, he say, and white men kill many buffalo for no reason. Indian Territory not have enough animals now to support the Comanche. He say his tribe must walk with head bowed, take handouts from Indian agents like Aitcheson.'

Everett's hands were cuffed in front of him, but he spurred his horse suddenly and it moved forward. Amos grabbed the reins and stopped it. Everett looked at Ten Bears and nodded towards the packhorse. 'You can be rich,' he said. He turned to Sugarfoot. 'Tell him there's a lotta dough in them saddle-bags. Tell him he can have half of it. Tell him he and his men will never starve again. Buy anything they want, anywhere – food, weapons, anything. All he has to do is give me a rifle and let me kill these two. They can hold you here, let you go in a while.' Sugarfoot didn't react and he raised his voice. 'Tell him!'

Ten Bears watched as Everett spoke and appeared to regard him with a detached curiousity. He looked at Sugarfoot and said something.

Sugarfoot said, 'He want to know what Stark say.'

'Translate it,' Amos replied.

'Everything he say?'

'Word for word,' Amos replied.

After Sugarfoot had translated Ten Bears walked his horse until he was level with Everett. He looked into his eyes for a moment, then went to the horse with the money. He opened the flap of one of the saddlebags and took out a bundle of dollars. He riffled through these, studied the portrait of President Grant, and grunted. He spoke briefly to Sugarfoot, put the bundle back and rode to where Everett was. He said something to him and returned to where the other Comanches were.

'He asked me to ask you about the dollars,' Sugarfoot said. 'He say picture of man on bill is the Great White Father, is not so?'

'Yes, Ulysses S. Grant,' Amos replied. 'The last president. He was succeeded by Rutherford B. Hayes last year.'

Sugarfoot translated and Ten Bears spoke again.

'Ten bears say if Great White Father's dollar paper is same as his treaty paper it is without value.' Sugarfoot pointed to Everett. 'He also say he understand we have trouble with this man. Says he thinks many white men are without honour, and says this man is one of these. He say he is low to try to trade paper for his life and freedom. He will let us go on, says he hopes Stark is hanged.'

'Tell him we're grateful for that,' Amos said.

'I will, *mi amigo*,' Sugarfoot said, 'but I had not finished translating what he say.'

'Sorry, Sugarfoot,' Amos said. 'Go on.'

'Ten Bears say we have three horses without riders. Say he trade our safe passage through Comanche land for these.'

'Tell him we agree,' Amos said.

Sugarfoot translated and Ten Bears put his arm across his chest, waved outward, and spoke again. 'He say, *go in peace*,' Sugarfoot said.

It had been a long ride and we were more than a little saddle-weary when we arrived in Buffalo Falls. We'd passed through the remainder of Comanche territory without further incident, and crossed the Red River at mid-morning. Apart for a short chow-stop in the late afternoon, when we got into town we'd ridden for almost ten hours.

The three of us stopped off at the office, where Sam Cole stood on the boardwalk to meet us.

Amos took Stark to a cell, then came out and brought the former marshal up to date.

'Well, I've gotta congratulate you fellas on a helluva job,' Cole said afterwards. 'I'll wire the circuit judge in Hamilton tonight. He should be able to arrange Stark's trial for sometime next week.'

'The Fargo man who was gutshot, he OK?' I asked.

'Yeah, name's Lionel Grant, he's recovering at Doc Taylor's. Doc says he'll most likely pull through.'

'You think he'll be fit enough to give evidence against Stark?' Amos asked.

'Sure of it,' Cole replied.

'Good,' Amos said. 'Stark might try to claim his brother Jeb did the killings. Might say they'd nothing to do with him.'

'Won't wash,' Cole said. 'Not from what Grant said when he spoke to you at McElhose's store. Case is clear cut.'

'Yeah, we think so,' Amos replied, then nodded to the gelding carrying the saddlebags with the cash. 'Sam, would you take care of the office a bit longer while we chase up Thoroughgood? Like to have him put the cash in his safe.'

'Sure, Amos,' Cole replied. 'And he's going to

be mighty pleased to see you.' He gave a wry smile. 'Or, more accurately, the dough. Told me the trail boss cleaned him out when he drew wages for the outfit that arrived the day you left. Another big drive's due in next week. He'll be needing it.'

'This lot of drovers give you any trouble?' Amos asked.

'One or two are peeved at the new statute. But they all gave up their irons. Oh, all except one, little Mexican fella called Carlos Mandia. Said he was going to see his fiancée who stays with his brother and his wife. They're homesteaders, live five miles north-west of here.'

'You seen him in town since?' Amos asked.

'No, the ramrod, Chuck Parker, is due to leave Monday morning. Expect he'll be back before then.'

'Know if he's a troublemaker?' I asked.

'Mandia? No, I don't think so. Might get a little rambunctious when he's liquored up, like most cowpunchers, but I've never had to spoke his wheel.'

'Good,' Amos replied. 'Well, we'd better get along and see Thoroughgood. Shouldn't be long.'

We rode on to McLehose's store, where

Sugarfoot dismounted and shook our hands. 'Be good to ride with you, *mi amigos,*' he said. 'If you need tracker again, come see me.'

'Been good riding with you, too, Sugarfoot,' Amos said. 'We couldn't have got Stark if you hadn't climbed that bluff and flushed him out.' He patted the rump of the horse carrying the money. 'The bank's paying a reward for the return of this cash. We'll see you get your share.'

'Really, *mi amigos*? You share with me?'

'Sure thing, Sugarfoot. Five thousand dollars. Just over sixteen hundred each.'

Sugarfoot looked thunderstruck and was silent for a moment. When he eventually caught his breath, he said, 'Sixteen hundred dollars! I be a rich man.'

'Ain't that much for what you done,' I said. 'You deserve it.'

Sugarfoot beamed. 'I can go to my mother in Indian Territory. She live further west from where we were yesterday. Maybe I buy homestead in Texas. Bring her here with me.'

'You surely can,' Amos said. 'Be a new start for you.'

'You good men, *mi amigos. Muchas gracias.*'

13

When we got to the bank it was closed. Thoroughgood heard us knocking and came to the window, then opened the door and ushered us in. We took the saddle-bags with us and went to his office, where he put the money on his desk and counted it before transferring it the safe.

'It's all there,' he said.

'Didn't give 'em time to spend any,' Amos said.

'You did an excellent job, gentlemen, and the bank is very grateful. You'll receive a five-thousand-dollar reward, two thousand five hundred each. I'll wire the Dodge office tomorrow to let them know it's here. They'll then authorize payment. Only a formality.'

'The reward, it's paid in cash?' Amos asked.

'Of course.'

'Fine,' Amos replied. 'Only it'll be split *three* ways. We had a tracker with us. Wouldn't have got your money but for his help.'

'Oh, I see,' Thoroughgood replied. 'I'll see the reward's made up accordingly.'

He took a cigar from a humidor on his desk, then bit off the end and lit it.

'Did you arrest any of the men?'

'Yes, one. We ran them down to a canyon in Indian Territory. They'd a hideout there and we had to shoot it out. Five killed. The one who surrendered is called Everett Stark. Brought him in for trial.'

'Good,' said Thoroughgood. 'You'll wire the circuit judge? Arrange for the trial?'

'Sam Cole's gonna wire him tonight. We've a witness, Fargo guard called Lionel Grant.'

'Yes, I know,' Thoroughgood replied. 'The man who's recovering at Doc Taylor's. How is he?'

'Sam Cole says he should make a full recovery. We're on our way to see him now.'

Doc Taylor was sitting on his porch reading the *Examiner* when we arrived at his house minutes later. He put down his paper when he saw us, stood up and extended his hand. 'Marshal Kane, Deputy Fisher. Good to see you. I passed your office a little while ago. Sam Cole was there. He told me you were back.'

We shook his hand and Amos said, 'We've just come from the bank. Thought we'd come over and see how Mr Grant's doing.'

'He's still quite weak,' Taylor said. 'He's been able to take liquids, though, and is improving. I'm sure he'll be his old self before long.'

He led us through to a little annexe that had been tacked on at the back of the house. A short corridor gave access to two rooms, one at either side. Taylor showed us into the one on the left, where Grant lay on a bed near a window.

'Lionel,' Taylor said, 'couple of visitors for you.'

Grant's eyes were closed but he wasn't asleep. He opened them and focused for a moment. He brightened visibly when he recognized us and shifted himself higher on the pillows. 'Howdy, Marshal, Deputy. Doc told me you'd gone after the men who shot me. You catch them?'

'We did, Lionel,' Amos replied. 'Brought their leader in for trial. Fella called Everett Stark.'

'You got just the one?'

'We killed the others in a shootout.'

'Oh. Well, can't say I'm sorry about that, because I ain't.'

'We've wired the circuit judge,' Amos said. 'Gonna try and fix Stark's trial for next week. We'd like to have you there as a witness. Think you'll be able to manage?'

'I ain't near bad as I was, Marshal. And I'm gettin' better every day. You bet I'll be there. Team of wild horses won't stop me.'

At noon the next day Amos and I were at the office when Sophia McLehose knocked at the door. She entered with the lunch basket, which she placed on the table. She looked pale and fraught, and appeared to find it difficult to hold our gaze when she spoke.

'Good day, Mr Kane, Mr Fisher,' she said. 'I'm glad to see you're both back again unharmed. I gather you caught the men who robbed the train.'

'We did, Sophia,' Amos replied.

'I heard you were involved in a gunfight, and that only one man survived.' She hesitated. 'I was told you have that man in custody.'

'We do, Sophia, yes.'

'Is your prisoner Everett Stark?' she asked.

'Yes ma'am, it is.'

'May I speak to him, please?' She nodded to the basket. 'I could take his lunch through, if you like.'

'You know Stark's a killer? That he's due at

court next week on a charge of robbery and murder?'

'I've heard that, yes,' she replied. 'I'd still like to speak to him if I may.'

'OK. Luke'll take you through. Five minutes is all the time I can give you, though.'

'That will be fine, Mr Kane. Thank you very much.'

I picked up Stark's lunch and escorted Sophia through. Everett Stark stood beside the bunk in one of the back office's two cells. He looked up and saw Sophia, then smiled and rose to his feet.

'Sophia, sweetheart,' he said. 'Ain't you a vision.'

'I asked if I could see you,' she said. 'The marshals have given me five minutes. I'm sorry to call during your lunch.'

Stark's expression changed to one of sarcasm. He looked at me and said, 'Mighty nice of them,' He turned again to Sophie and beamed. 'Don't worry, sweetheart,' he said. 'I'd much rather talk to you than eat. I'll get it later.'

I opened his cell and put his meal on the table, then locked the door behind me and took a stool from the empty cell next to his. I placed it near the bars. 'You can sit here, Miss McLehose,' I said, then left.

When I returned, Amos shook his head. 'What does she see in that four-flusher?'

'I think he made a big impression when he first came here,' I replied. 'Said he was interested in ranching down near the Gulf. Her eyes lit up that night when she told her father about it.'

'But she's got to know now that that was a bluff. He wasn't really interested in ranching.'

'Figure maybe he done a good job of persuadin' her. I've been thinking how she was that night at her father's place. She's not long returned from staying with her uncle, remember. Could be she's been happier there.'

'Think so?'

'Yeah, I do. When McLehose mentioned his wife's death she didn't like him talking about it. Got up and left the room the moment he raised the subject. It's possible Buffalo Falls has painful memories for her.'

'So Stark sweet-talks her into thinkin' he's going there to down stakes, and maybe she thinks he's good husband material?'

'Pretty much how I figure it,' I replied.

'Well she certainly seems to have set her hat at him.'

'Looked that way the night I seen 'em outside the store.'

Amos looked at the clock. 'Well, I hate to break up their party,' he said, 'but time's up. She's had her five minutes.'

Sophia came back through and picked up the empty basket. 'Thank you, Mr Kane, I appreciate your letting me see him,' she said.

'Sorry if he's disillusioned you in any way, Sophia,' Amos replied.

Sophia looked at Amos and I saw a flash of anger in her face.

'Please don't take this the wrong way, Marshal, but I think you may be the one who's taken the wrong view of things.'

'I'm sorry, ma'am, I don't get your meaning.'

'Your prisoner, Everett Stark,' she said. 'I believe him to be innocent of murder.'

'I really don't know how you could think that,' Amos replied.

'Don't you? Then let me tell you why. Everett Stark has ridden with his brother Jeb since he was freed from Yaqui prison in Arizona in January. The reason he did so was to try and keep his brother out of trouble. He stayed with his brother and the men who rode with him and was coerced into doing the things he did. He tried to persuade Jeb not to carry out the robberies both here and at Sweetwater.'

'Everett told you this hogwash? Amos said. 'Pardon me, Sophia, but if you really believe that, you're deceiving yourself.'

'I hadn't finished,' she said.

'Pardon me,' Amos replied. 'Carry on.'

'As I understand it, the only witness to the shooting of the Wells Fargo men is the gentleman who's recovering at Doctor Taylor's.'

'The Wells Fargo men on the train, ma'am, yes,' Amos replied. 'There were two other Fargo men killed at Sweetwater, and an accountant.'

'But there was no witness to those killings?'

'No, ma'am, there wasn't.'

'And in order to convict Mr Stark for murder, you have to have someone who witnessed him carrying out the crime, is that not so?'

Amos nodded. 'Yes, that's true. The witness to Wednesday's shootings is Mr Grant, the Fargo man you mentioned.'

'And he saw Everett Stark killing the men at the train?'

'Yes, ma'am, he did.'

Sophia walked to the door and opened it. 'I think you'll find Mr Grant is wrong, Marshal. Jeb did the shooting. Everett is innocent.'

Amos said, 'Well, that's something that'll have to be decided at trial.'

Sophia said nothing. She left, banging the door behind her.

14

Lionel Grant had to be helped into the Houston Hotel's barroom, which was closed for the morning and stood in for the courtroom. Doc Taylor gave his patient the use of a Bath chair, an awkward-looking three-wheeled contraption that Amos and I lifted in from the street.

The saloon was packed with townspeople, many seated on chairs which had been set up in rows. Sophia McLehose and her father sat next to a pillar near the back.

The judge, a short, bespectacled man called Parker J. Whitfield, consulted his notes behind a desk Breen had brought through from his office. There was no prosecutor and the defence lawyer, William Penrose, sat next to Everett. I pushed Grant to the front and he was sworn in.

'Mr Grant, as the only witness to the shootings last Wednesday, may I take your statement now?' Whitfield said.

'Yes, your honour,' Grant replied. 'Me and three other men were in the armoured Fargo coach when the train was stopped fifteen miles outside town. The robbers put cloths soaked in kerosene in the air vents. Lit 'em. We couldn't breathe, had to open the doors. That's when they shot us.'

'Who shot you, Mr Grant?'

'Like I told the marshals when I was brought in, I couldn't see all the men. Just the ones in front. Two big fellas. Man with scar and another one.'

'The other man, can you see him in this court?'

'Yes, your honour,' Grant replied. 'He's sitting in the front row.'

'Mr Everett Stark?'

'Yes, your honour.'

'Defence Counsel, you wish to examine the witness?'

Penrose stood up. 'Thank you, your honour. Mr Grant, you say you saw Jeb and Everett Stark, but you couldn't see the other men, is that true?'

'Yes, sir, it is.'

'Why couldn't you see the other men?'

'Because when the door of the coach was slid

open they were at either side, out of view. But the Stark brothers were right outside. They had their rifles aimed and commenced firing the second they saw us. We didn't have a chance. We were choked up from the smoke and our eyes were streaming.'

'I take it that when the door was opened the smoke billowed out?'

'Yes, sir, it did.'

'Where were you standing in the coach in relation to your colleagues?'

'On the left.'

'And on what side was Jeb Stark standing when you looked out?'

'On the left.'

'You were on the left side looking out and saw Jeb shooting?'

'Yes, sir, it was him who shot me.'

Penrose thumbed the inside of his jacket lapels. 'So, there was smoke billowing from the coach, and your eyes were streaming. Yet you managed to see not only the man who shot you, but were also able to spot his brother shooting from the other side?'

'Yes, sir, that's what I saw.'

'Mr Grant, with the smoke and your impaired vision, isn't it possible you saw only one man with a rifle – the man who shot you? My client maintains he didn't shoot anyone. He did, in fact, try to restrain his brother.'

'I know what I saw, mister. Yeah, my eyes were watering and there was smoke, that's true. But I saw both men shoot, saw it clear as day.'

Judge Whitfield held up his hands. 'That'll do counsellor, I've heard enough. Thanks, Mr Grant. Marshal Kane, I'll take your testimony now.'

Amos took the stand. He told the court about Coyote Canyon and the sustained fire we took from the Stark brothers and their men before overcoming them and arresting Everett.

Whitfield dismissed Amos and wrote something on a piece of foolscap. 'Everett Stark,' he said. 'It is the finding of this court that you were fully complicit in the murders of three Fargo men at Pine Ridge, the attempted murder of Mr Lionel Grant, and the theft of fifty thousand dollars. Nothing I've heard from your counsel here today persuades me otherwise. We have no absolute proof of your involvement of the killings at Sweetwater, but there is no doubt in my mind that you were involved in that crime also. I find you guilty of these charges and sentence you to hang at Yaqui Prison, at a time to be decided by the prison governor.'

He brought down his gavel and said, 'Court's adjourned.'

I looked to the back of the court and saw Sophia McLehose dab her eyes with a lace handkerchief. Moments later she and her father left.

The court was cleared. Amos and I returned to the office and put Stark back in his cell.

The next day Amos and I were in the office when Thoroughgood stopped by. He told us the reward had been approved by the Dodge office and that the money could be claimed at the bank.

'Luke and I decided to leave our share in the bank for now,' Amos told the banker. 'Luke will drop by later this morning to pick up the tracker's share, if that's OK.'

'That's fine,' Thoroughgood replied. 'I'll make sure it's waiting. Has Mr Stark been transferred to Yaqui Prison yet?'

'County sheriff and his deputies collect him tomorrow,' Amos replied.

'You'll be glad to be relieved of responsibility for his custody?'

'We will,' Amos replied. 'One of us has to be in the office at all times right now.'

Thoroughgood doffed his hat. 'Well, thanks again for a job well done, gentlemen. See you soon, Mr Fisher. Good day, Mr Kane.'

At noon I was leaving to pick up Sugarfoot's share of the reward when Sophia McElhose came into the office. She carried a tray on which were our meals and a pot of coffee. I was surprised to see her, as ever since her last visit the chow had been brought by her father.

She placed the tray on the table and looked directly at Amos.

'I was very rude the last time I saw you, Mr Kane,' she said. 'And I'd like to say sorry. I wanted to believe in Mr Stark's innocence. I know it was stupid of me to think that way. Will you accept my apology?'

'Of course,' Amos replied. 'It's nice to see you again.'

She indicated the tray. 'I've brought some cold cuts of ham with sweet potatoes,' she said. 'Also fresh coffee to save you making it.' She took two cups from the tray and began pouring. 'You both better drink it before it's cold.'

'Sorry, Miss McLehose,' I said. 'Just pour the one cup for now. I'm just leaving: got to see Mr Thoroughgood at the bank.'

Sophia stopped pouring the second cup. 'Oh, I see,' she said. 'You'll be gone long?'

'Coffee'll probably be cold when I get back,' I

said. 'I'll make some more. Thanks, though, I appreciate the gesture.'

I left and went to the bank. Thoroughgood had the money waiting and I took it to McLehose's. Sugarfoot was loading a wagon when I arrived and he smiled when he saw me.

I handed him the envelope. 'Your share of the reward, Sugarfoot,' I said.

'*Muchos gracias, mi amigo,*' he replied. 'I am nearly finished this work now. I told Mr McLehose about the money and he tell me it OK to leave when I get it.'

'You're bringing your mother back to Texas?'

'*Sí, mi amigo,* I go now, today. I get her, find homestead. She live here with me.'

'I wish you good luck, my friend.'

I shook hands with Sugarfoot and walked back towards the office. I was almost at the Houston Hotel when Breen came out and saw me. His face was flushed and he looked quite perturbed.

15

Breen seemed relieved to see me. 'Ah, Mr Fisher. Thank God you're here,' he said. 'It's one of Chuck Parker's drovers, a Mexican, name of Mandia. Didn't go with the others last week when they left to return south. He's in the bar and he's drunk. Armed with a pistol. Threatening to shoot the place up.'

'How long's he been drinking?'

'Couldn't say. Elias, my barman, only served him a couple of shots. He must have been on the bottle before he got here. Are you going to get Mr Kane?'

'No,' I replied. 'He can't leave the office. We still have Stark in custody.'

'Oh, yes. Sorry,' Breen said. 'Can you deal with the Mexican, Mr Fisher?'

I hadn't taken the Sharps, but had my Army

Colt on my hip. 'Sure,' I replied, then followed him into the hotel.

When I entered Mandia stood alone at the bar with his back to me. The barman and the only three customers in the room stood well clear at the other end. The Mexican was hunched over the bar counter, mumbling something in Spanish. He straightened up and I saw he had a Peacemaker in his hand.

He looked at his reflection in the bar mirror and waved the pistol. 'I'll kill him,' he said. 'I'll kill her, too. How could they do this? How could *he* do this? To me, Carlos, his only brother?'

Mandia turned around. He was about thirty, slightly built, and had a pockmarked face. Tears were streaming down his cheeks. He pointed the pistol at the ceiling and waved it again. 'I should have killed them,' he said.

I had my Colt out and aimed at him. 'I'll be obliged if you put down that gun,' I said. 'Do it now, else I'll shoot you.'

Mandia looked in my direction and appeared to register my presence for the first time. His eyes were glazed, and he swayed as he stood.

'Who are you, a friend of Chuck Parker? Tell him I drive cattle no more. I gonna go back. Kill her, kill him.'

'I'm Luke Fisher, deputy marshal. You're not going to kill anyone. Do as I say, drop that pistol.'

Mandia dropped his arm and held the Peacemaker loosely at his side. He shook his head. 'I kill myself, then.'

I realized that the man posed no immediate danger to me or anyone else in the room. I began to reason with him. 'No one needs to get hurt, you included. Give me the gun.'

He appeared not to have heard me. 'I get to my brother's house after cattle drive,' he said. 'My fiancée stay there, supposed to be waiting for me. Find her in bed with my brother, Miguel. His wife, Maria, leave him two days before I get back. She discover they are lovers. Take *los niños* with her and go back to Mexico. Alameda, my fiancée, she say want to stay with my brother. She say she love him, don't care for me no more.' He shook his head again. 'I no kill them, *señor*, I shoot myself. Be better for everyone, no?'

'Your name is Carlos, that right?' I asked.

'*Sí, señor.*'

'Carlos, I understand that what happened with your fiancée has made you angry. But killing yourself just ain't the answer.'

'Life without Alameda be a life I no think I can live.'

'What about your sister-in-law, Maria? She'll be be feeling low, like you. Think she'll want to end it all? You said she's got children?'

'*Sí, señor,* she has two. A boy and a girl.'

'She's gotta consider them, hasn't she?'

'Yes, *señor,* is true.'

'The three of them have got a future, Carlos, and so have you. C'mon, give me the pistol. We'll get you a room upstairs. You'll feel better tomorrow.'

Mandia seemed to sober up. He reversed the gun and offered it to me, butt first. 'Sorry I make a scene, *señor,*' he said. 'I been drinking for most of last week. I tired. I angry. I no really want to kill Alameda or my brother.'

I asked Breen to give him a room and we put him to bed. The minute he hit the sack he was out like a light. 'He just needs to sleep it off,' I told Breen. 'Ain't likely to give you any more trouble. When he wakes up he'll most probably accept what's happened and get on with it. We'll keep his pistol at the office for a while, anyway. Just to be on the safe side.'

'Grateful to you, Mr Fisher,' Breen replied. 'For a while there I thought someone was gonna get hurt.'

*

When I reached the office the door was slightly open. I entered and saw Amos slumped over the desk. I pulled him up and he gave a low moan and lolled back again. I checked for signs of injury, found none, then went through to the back. Stark's cell was open and he was gone. I checked the gun safe and saw that a Winchester, two Colts and a couple of boxes of shells were missing. The keys to the gun safe were still in the lock.

Amos gave another groan and moved a little. I placed a cushion under his head and put coffee on the stove. It was then that it hit me: *Sophia*. Unusually, she'd brought coffee in with the chow. She'd poured it right away, too, and had been quite insistent that we should drink it before it got cold. But only Amos had had a cup. I remembered she'd asked how long I'd be gone.

The cup Amos had drunk from lay on the desk. It was empty. I lifted it to my nose and detected a faint whiff of spice. Whatever she'd put in the coffee had been enough to knock Amos out. She must have waited until he was unconscious, then taken the keys from his belt and released Everett. Stark had helped himself to the guns and ammo before they left.

Amos stirred. 'Whassgoingon?' he said. I

poured some strong black coffee into a mug and took it to him. I managed to get him to swallow some. A few minutes later he still looked groggy, but was able to talk.

'Everett's escaped,' I told him. 'Looks like Sophia put something in the coffee she brought. When you fell unconscious she took your keys and unlocked his cell. He's hightailed it. Taken a rifle, pistols and ammo with him.'

He took another slug of coffee. 'How long's he been gone?' he said.

'I left the office forty minutes ago.' I said. 'Can't be longer than that.'

He stood up and put a hand to his head. 'Feel as though I've just drunk a bottle of hooch.'

'You gonna be OK to move?'

'Reckon so. Just a little unsteady. Do you think Sophia went with him?'

'I think it's likely. Only one way to find out, though.'

'You're right,' Amos replied. 'We'd better see McLehose.'

'I'm sorry, Mr Kane, she's not here,' McLehose said when we spoke to him in his storeroom a few minutes later. His shoulders were slumped and he looked downcast. He raised his hands in a gesture of exasperation. 'I blame myself, of course,' he said. 'I knew there was something between her and Stark soon after he arrived. She seemed to have fallen for him pretty hard. When he told her he intended buying a ranch in the Gulf, she was in a swoon. I think she imagined starting a new life there. You see, after her mother died I sent her off to stay with my brother Phillip for a couple of months. When she came back she was moody and morose. Told me she preferred San Antonio to here. Spent as much time with Phillip as she did with me.'

'But after the train was robbed and Stark disappeared,' Amos asked, 'didn't she realize he'd been spinning her a yarn?'

'I think she wanted to believe that at least part of what he said was true. About him being interested in her and going to San Antonio, I mean.'

'Think that's where they're headed now?' I asked.

McLehose nodded to the corral at the back of the store. 'Two horses been taken,' he said. 'Sophia's palomino and my appaloosa. I think if he persuaded her he was still interested in ranching, they might've gone south.'

'Well they can't have got much of a lead,' Amos said. 'We'd better get after them.'

'There's one other thing,' McLehose said.

He went to a shelf and shifted a clay pot. He took an opaque bottle from behind and brought it over. 'Laudanum,' he said. 'I found it in a cupboard in the kitchen this morning. I'm sorry, Mr Kane, but that's what Sophia used to drug your coffee. You may remember she fetched it from Doc Taylor's the day Mr Grant was brought here. She must've forgotten to return it.'

16

We briefed Sam Cole and he agreed to watch the office and telegraph the county sheriff. This wire would be relayed to all towns south of Buffalo Falls, and there was a chance a marshal or sheriff in one of those places might intercept Everett and Sophia.

That didn't seem all that likely, though. Even accounting for the time spent at McLehose's and apprising Sam Cole of what was happening, we didn't think they'd be that far ahead. When Amos and I left Buffalo Falls just after one o'clock, we reckoned there were only ten miles between us.

We soon rode beyond the places we'd reconnoitred the day before Stark robbed the train. After the dry scrubland and buttes, the trail led through a large forested area, where we began to give their tracks more attention.

'We've been able to follow their signs so far,' Amos said. 'But we'll need to be careful they don't go off trail. Might try to throw us now that it winds through these woods.'

'Also be an ideal place to set up an ambush,' I said.

'I don't think that's likely,' Amos replied. 'Despite what's happened, I think Sophia's only motivation was Everett's death sentence. She's smitten with him and believes he ain't really a killer. To keep her thinkin' that way, he'd have to avoid shooting us in a trap.'

'But he took weapons from the gun safe. Surely she saw that?'

'Yeah, she would've. Yet he didn't kill me. Why?'

'Think he was gonna shoot you? Maybe she persuaded him not to?'

'Remember what Stark said to Ten Bears, the Comanche chief?'

' "Give me rifle and I'll kill those two?" '

'Exactly. I was out for the count. He had the guns and the opportunity. But he didn't take it. He knew I'd come after him.'

'But once she'd freed him why worry about her?' I said.

'Thought about that, too. Don't for a moment think he returns her feelings. Which leaves one other thing.'

'What's that?' I asked.

'He thinks she might prove useful.'

'He might use her as a hostage?'

'Yeah. He'll keep goin' south for a while, as long as he thinks he needs her. Lull her into thinkin' he genuinely wants what she wants.'

'Then he'll abandon her and go his own way?'

'Likely,' Amos replied. 'But we've got to catch up with them before that happens.'

The forest gave way to rolling grassland, and still Everett and Sophia's tracks were visible on the trail south. In the late afternoon we came to a staging post which was manned by a Boone & Bannerman agent. The man was seated on a stoop in front of the post's cabin when we approached. He stood up when he saw us.

'Afternoon, gents,' he said. 'There's a trough out back, if your horses need water. Pump, too. You can fill your canteens.'

Amos and I dismounted.

'Appreciate that,' I said. We led our mounts to the pasture at the rear of the cabin and let them drink their fill at the trough. The man followed us. He mopped his brow with his bandanna, then stuffed it in his pocket.

'Hot, ain't it?'

'It is,' I replied.

He scratched his head. 'Funny thing,' he said. 'Apart from cattle drives and stages I don't get to see many folks. Then this afternoon two sets of riders headin' south within an hour of each other.'

'Other riders you saw,' Amos said, 'were they a man and a woman?'

'Yeah, young girl, pretty. Wore Levis and a checked shirt. Man was a tall fella with a thin moustache. You know 'em?'

'Yeah, we do. Did they stop for any length of time?'

'Only to water their horses and fill their canteens.'

'They say anything?' I asked.

'Fella asked me how far to the next town.'

'How far is it?'

'Little place called Jasper Creek. Forty or fifty miles.'

'And you say they passed by an hour ago?' Amos asked.

The man stroked his chin and nodded. 'Couldn't be more than that.'

We mounted up and Amos tipped his hat. 'Well, thanks, friend,' he said. 'You've been mighty helpful.'

The light was beginning to fade and we decided to look for a place to camp for the night. We crossed a dried-out riverbed and picked our way through some dense mesquite for a half-hour or so, then Amos reined in his paint. He took his binoculars from his saddle pack and focused on the ground ahead. He gave me the glasses and pointed to a depression a half-mile further on.

'Look ahead to where the ground dips,' he said. 'Someone's lit a fire.'

I took the glasses and saw a sheltered hollow ahead. There were clumps of cottonwoods dotted around, and through gaps in the trees I could make out a firelight's flicker.

'Look's like they're gettin' ready to camp,' I said. 'We must have made better time than we thought.'

'Strange he's lit a fire, though,' Amos said. 'Bound to realize it'll draw attention.'

' 'Less it ain't Stark.'

'Only one way to find out,' Amos said. 'Better hobble the horses here and go on foot. Get close without alerting them.'

The two of us took our time and covered the ground to the hollow as stealthily as we could. One particular stand of cottonwoods reached right to the rim of the depression, so we dropped to the ground and wriggled through on our hands and knees.

When we reached the rim we saw Sophia at one side of the clearing, rubbing the muzzle of her palomino. She looked nervous and was watching Everett, who stood near the fire speaking to one of three other men. The man Stark was talking to was American; he was taller and heavier than his two companions and wore a Confederate Army Stetson. The other two were dark-complexioned, and looked like Mexicans. They were bearded, heavy-set and wore bandoleers across their chests. All three men had gunbelts with twin holsters and Army Colts, positioned butt forward. Their horses stood near by, and each saddle scabbard carried a Winchester carbine.

'Didn't think I'd run into you this far west, Barney,' we heard Everett say. 'Last time we met you were in Indian Territory.'

'Yeah I was,' the man called Barney replied. 'Still am. Me, Santos and Rodriguez been supplying two renegade Comanche chiefs, Bald Eagle and Whispering Jack. We loot where we can.

Guns, horses, supplies. Anything the redskins want. Head back to the Nations and trade for buffalo hides.'

Barney paused and gave Sophia a quizzical look. 'Where's Jeb and the rest of your outfit?'

'Had a run-in with a couple of marshals in a cowtown up the trail aways. They killed Jeb and the others. Fixin' to hang me. I escaped, but they ain't far behind.'

'I see,' Barney said. He glanced again at Sophia and a lecherous look came over his face. 'Fine-looking travellin' companion you've got, Ev. She your woman?'

Stark didn't answer. 'Them marshals I told you about, Barney,' he said. 'Won't be long before they catch up. I gotta keep moving. Need me a stake, too. Can you spare fifty bucks? You know I'll get it back to you.'

'You an' me have shared a few trails, Ev. But you should know I make a habit of never giving anything less I get collateral. Which way you headed, anyway?'

'Going west, to Calif—' He caught himself. He looked over at Sophia. 'Going south to the Gulf Coast. Like to buy me a stake in a ranch.'

'Fifty dollars ain't enough for that, Ev,' Barney said. 'What about the woman?'

'What about her?' Everett replied.

'I asked if she was your woman,' Barney said.

'Not exactly, no.' Everett replied. 'She's someone who's been helpful to me.'

'Whispering Jack got a real fondness for blondes, Ev,' Barney said. 'Give you five hundred dollars for her. Get you to California. That's where you're really headed, ain't it?'

Sophia had remained with her palomino throughout the exchange, but now she walked over and took Stark's arm. 'It was a mistake to stop, Everett,' she said. 'These men are despicable.' She turned to Barney with fury in her eyes. 'What do you think I am, horseflesh?' She turned and went back to her horse. 'I want to leave, Everett,' she said. 'Now.'

Barney laughed. 'Well, she's got some spirit, Ev. Whispering Jack'll like that. What about it? Five hundred bucks. Would get you a new start.'

We could see Everett chewing it over. He was quiet for a moment. He looked at Sophia, then back at Barney. 'She's got a fine palomino,' he said. 'What about seven-fifty for 'em both?'

Barney laughed again. 'Still horsetrading, huh, Ev? OK, I'll give you six hundred.'

Everett turned to Sophia, whose expression was a mixture of astonishment and terror. He shrugged his shoulders. 'Sorry, sweetheart,' he said. 'But needs must when the devil drives.'

17

Sophia ran to her horse and had swung on to the saddle when the two Mexicans caught her and dragged her to the ground. She screamed and kicked and succeeded in hitting the shorter of the two of them in the solar plexus. He fell to his knees, winded. The other man grabbed her by the hair and hauled her towards Barney, who went to his horse and brought a rope. While the Mexican held Sophia, he trussed her arms and legs.

'Sassy, ain't ya?' Barney said when he'd done. He went to his saddle and took a leather pouch. He counted out 600 dollars and handed them to Stark. 'Here you are, Ev,' he said, 'looks like she'll be worth every penny.'

Amos and I had seen enough. Our rifles were

with the horses, but we still had our Colts and they were fully loaded. We stood up and strode into the clearing with pistols drawn. 'I'll watch Everett and Barney,' Amos said quietly. 'You cover the Mexicans.'

Sophia lay near the fire in the middle of the clearing. Everett was getting ready to mount the appaloosa on the left. Barney was between Stark and the two Mexicans, who stood on the right.

'Be obliged if none of you would move,' Amos said. 'Everett, stay where you are. Walk an inch closer to that horse and I'll shoot you.'

Everett stopped, but his hand hovered near his holster. Barney looked surprised but quickly regained his composure. He gave Amos a defiant look. 'Think two of you are a match for four of us, Marshal?' he said. 'It is marshal, ain't it? You're the men who are chasing Stark?'

'We are,' Amos replied. 'And we'll shoot the four of you before you've a chance to clear leather,' Amos said. 'Try anything fancy and you'll learn that the hard way.'

'You'd get Stark, sure,' Barney replied. 'But when you were gunnin' him, I'd get you.'

'What makes you so sure I'd aim for Stark first?' Amos said.

Barney laughed. 'The situation is what you'd

call a stand-off, ain't it?'

I looked at the Mexicans. They were rolling on their heels, getting ready to move. They looked to be no strangers to gunfights and were likely to be quick on the draw. Question was, even with the advantage of my Colt cocked and ready, could I drop both of them before they drew their pistols?

Any advantage we had, though, was lost the next moment. The fire sparked suddenly and spat out an ember the size of a dime. It hit the back of Sophia's shirt and she screamed and rolled on to her back in an effort to extinguish it.

This split-second distraction was enough. Everett and Barney had their pistols pulled before Amos could react. Barney had both guns out and got off a shot with the pistol in his left hand before Amos returned fire. Barney's round flew a fraction wide. Amos's aim was deadly accurate, however; the bullet hit Barney's forehead with a sharp crack.

But this had given Everett time to aim and squeeze the trigger. Amos bobbed down quickly, and it was a reaction that saved his life; Everett's round caught his Stetson and blew it off his head. Amos returned fire and the bullet hit Everett's chest; he twisted ninety degrees, seemed to hang for a moment, then fell.

I'd been luckier, meanwhile. The Mexican whom Sophia had winded didn't react by going for his guns right away. Instead, when the fire sparked he ducked as if it was a shot he'd heard.

The other man responded much faster.

Using a crossover draw, he managed to clear leather with both pistols before I shot and dropped him. His companion realized what was happening then, and he too went for his guns. The little Mexican had barely palmed his pistols when my round hit his chest. He gave a low moan and pitched forward into the dirt.

I went over to Sophia and cut the rope binding her. The ember had burned a hole in the back of her shirt, and I could see the flesh underneath was seared. I soaked my bandanna with water from one of the Mexican's canteens and placed it next to the blister.

'You OK, Sophia?' I asked.

She winced. 'Yes, Luke, thank you. I managed to shake off the worst of it when I rolled away from the fire.'

Amos helped her on to her palomino, and we led it and her father's appaloosa back to where our horses were tethered. Soon we had a fire going and some strong coffee on the brew. We poured Sophia a cup and when she took it I noticed that her hands were trembling.

'You both saved me from something incredibly sordid,' she said. 'I don't know how to begin to say thanks.'

'You don't have to,' Amos said.

'But I treated you terribly, Amos,' she said. 'I'm truly sorry. What I did was unforgivable. Putting laudanum in your coffee and drugging you. Then almost getting you killed.'

'Apology accepted, Sophia. And don't worry about the gunfight. Luke and I have faced worse odds.'

'No, I don't mean here,' she said. 'Back in your office.'

'Everett wanted to shoot me?' Amos said.

'Yes,' Sophia replied. 'When I unlocked the cell, he broke into your gun safe and was going to kill you with one of the pistols. I made him stop. I reminded him he'd said he hadn't taken part in the killings. I told him if he shot you that would make him a killer. He relented.'

'Then you saved my life,' Amos replied.

She started to cry. 'I'm glad of that, but ashamed of the other things I did.' She began to dab her eyes with her shirtsleeve. 'You were right, I've been deceiving myself from the very beginning. I was in love with him. I so wanted to believe what he told me.' Her shoulders shook and her sobbing got worse. 'Everett told me he cared for me. In the end, all I was worth to him was six hundred dollars.'

Amos went over and put a blanket around her. 'It's been an unsettling experience, Sophia,' he said. 'But put it behind you. Come on, you look done in. Better get some sleep. We've a long ride ahead of us tomorrow.'

18

At noon the next day we stopped at the Boone & Bannerman office we'd passed on the way south. Amos got the agent to wire the county sheriff and arrange for the bodies of Everett and the other men to be taken to the undertaker's at Jasper Creek. He also asked the man to telegraph Sam Cole and let him know we were on our way.

We reached Buffalo Falls a few hours later and took Sophia to her father. Our next stop was the office, where Sam was waiting for us.

'Got your wire, fellas,' he said. 'Sophia back at the store?'

'Yeah, she's with her father,' Amos replied.

'You ain't lookin' to prosecute her? Aiding and abetting?'

'No,' Amos replied. 'She was misguided. Had a

thing for Stark and was blinkered by his lies. But she saved my life. Everett was fixin' to shoot me when she sprung him. She persuaded him not to.'

'Yes, I think she's a good gal at heart,' Cole replied. 'Known her since she was a baby. Martha, her mother, was a heck of a fine woman, too.'

'Yeah, Mr McLehose told me about his wife,' Amos said.

Cole tipped his Stetson. 'Well, if you don't mind I'll get back to the little woman. Don't know why I should hurry, though. When I did this full time, she complained about me never being home. And when I'm home she complains about me sitting around the house. Can't win, huh?'

'You miss marshalling?' Amos asked.

'Tell the truth I do, Amos,' Cole replied. 'Didn't think I would, but I do. Helping you boys out has made me realize that.'

Next afternoon Amos and I were sitting on the boardwalk ruminating on events and thinking about our future. Amos leaned back and balanced his chair on its back legs.

'You know, Luke, what Sam Cole said yesterday got me thinking.'

'About him regretting retiring as marshal?' I replied.

'Yeah, exactly. Don't know about you, but I'm not sure about this job. Too much like the army.'

'Highs and lows, you mean?'

'Yeah, just that. At Fort Larned we'd be all over the place for days hunting renegades. Then for weeks it would be quiet. A few days ago we were out on the chase. Now we're sitting here waiting for something to happen.'

'What else could we do?'

'Got more than three thousand bucks reward money; we could head south, start us a business.'

'Not ranching?'

Amos laughed. 'Hell, no. Gave up on that idea, too. Got no affinity with steers. No, being here's given me a taste for town living.'

'We could open a bar, maybe. Or a store?'

'Yeah, something like that,' Amos replied. 'What do you think?'

'Yeah, I kinda like the idea. Spent too much of my life in the saddle. Be good to have a go at something else.'

As we spoke a buckboard made its way along Main Street towards us. The driver was a freckle-faced man who looked to be in his late twenties. Beside him was a dark-haired woman of about the same age. He reined the horse to a stop in front of the office, then stepped down and walked over.

He tipped his Stetson and pointed behind us. 'Pardon me, gents, I'm looking for Sam Cole, the town marshal. Is he in the office?'

'I took over from Sam Cole,' Amos said. 'A few weeks back. My name's Amos Kane. This here's my deputy, Luke Fisher.'

'Oh,' he said. He had a disappointed look on his face. 'I'm Tom Quincy. I was deputy marshal myself until a month or two ago. Gave it up and went to Richmond to fetch my fiancée Mary.' He nodded towards the young woman. 'Mary Abercombie; we're about to be married.'

Amos and I tipped our hats. 'Pleased to meet you, ma'am,' we said in unison.

Mary nodded shyly. 'Pleased to meet you, gentlemen.'

'I was hoping the post of deputy wouldn't be taken yet,' Quincy said. 'I took a chance in returning, you see. I don't have a job.'

Amos looked at me and winked. 'Well, you're coming here now is a bit of a coincidence. Luke and I are moving on.'

Quincy's face brightened visibly. 'You mean there's a vacancy for deputy marshal?' he asked.

'There is,' Amos replied. 'Marshal, too. And I fancy Sam Cole will be happy get his old job back. You know where he lives?'

'Sam Cole? Yes, Mr Kane, I do,' Quincy replied.

'Then go and tell him Luke and I are retiring as of tomorrow and he's marshal again. And you can take over as his deputy. Luke and I will let the town citizens' committee know later.'

Breen, Thoroughgood and Peabody met us in the lounge of the Houston Hotel early next morning. Sophia and her father sat with them.

'I'm sure I speak for all of us when I say we're sorry you're leaving,' Breen said. 'But we've done as you asked and reappointed Cole and Quincy to the office of marshal and deputy.'

Thoroughgood handed Amos and me each an envelope with the balance of the reward. 'I gather you're riding south?' he said.

'Yes, Luke and I are going to take a look at some of the towns growing up along the new southern railroad spur,' Amos replied. He held up his envelope. 'Figure we'll use this to start a business in one of them.'

'Well, whatever you decide on, I wish you every success,' Thoroughgood replied.

McLehose walked over and shook our hands. 'Sophia told me of her ordeal with Stark and those bandits. I can't begin to express my thanks to you both for saving her,' he said.

Sophia pressed forward and kissed us both on the cheek. 'And I would like to add something,' she said. 'My mother's death affected me deeply and I tried to shut it out by running to my Uncle Phillip. What happened has made me realize how much my mother sacrificed to make a new life for us here. I won't be returning to San Antonio. I'm going to stay here and help my father.' She kissed us again. 'God bless you both and thank you for everything.'

A few minutes later we said goodbye to everyone on the boardwalk outside. We were mounting up when Breen came over. 'Luke, I almost forgot,' he said. 'You may be interested to know that Carlos Mandia rode south to join Chuck Parker's outfit after all.'

Amos gave me a quizzical look.

'The Mexican I told you was threatening to kill himself,' I reminded him.

Amos nodded. 'Oh yeah, I remember.'

'Ah, yes, but the irony is that Carlos's ex-girlfriend Alameda left Miguel soon after,' Breen said. 'Went to Mexico. Miguel took off after her. Sold his homestead before he went. Guess who bought it?'

'No idea,' I replied.

'Your 'breed tracker, Sugarfoot. Brought his

mother here with him from Indian Territory.'

'Glad to hear that,' I said. 'He told us he was looking for a place to settle.'

'Yeah, that's great news,' Amos said. 'Everything panned out as he hoped it would.'

Breen extended his hand. 'Well, I'll say goodbye to you both and wish you the best of luck.'

We shook his hand, tipped our hats to the others, and began to ride out of town. The two of us had reached the junction of Main and Sixth Street when we saw Michelle and Rosamund waving to us from the boardwalk.

'Luke, *mon cher,* I 'ear you are leaving,' Michelle said.

'We are, Michelle, but I'll come back again sometime.'

'You will, *mon cher*?'

'Yes, I promise.'

Rosamund looked at Amos. 'You'll come and see me again sometime, too, won't you, Amos?' she said.

'I will, Rosamund.'

Michelle waved a lace handkerchief. '*Au revoir, mon cher,*' she called.

Rosamund waved a coloured fan. 'Goodbye, honey,' she said.

We waved back and rode on and then it hit me. I looked at Amos. 'See her *again*?'

'Visited her at the Alamo the night after you saw Michelle,' Amos said.

I snickered. 'You sly old devil.'

Amos grinned. 'Well you did say she wanted me to.'

'She seems happy you did.'

'Didn't give no complaint.'

We both began laughing. Then the two of us rode clear of Buffalo Falls and struck out for the south.